HEAD
IN THE SAND

ALSO BY DAMIEN BOYD

As the Crow Flies
Kickback

DAMIEN BOYD
HEAD IN THE SAND

THOMAS & MERCER

Published by Thomas & Mercer, Seattle

www.apub.com

Amazon, the Amazon logo, and Thomas & Mercer are trademarks of Amazon.com, Inc., or its affiliates.

ISBN-13: 978-1477821046
ISBN-10: 147782104X

Cover concept by Littera Designs
Cover created by bürosüd° München, www.buerosued.de

Library of Congress Control Number: 2014947408

Printed in the United States of America

For my parents, Michael and Diane

Prologue

To the casual observer she appeared alive and well, but anyone who knew her would tell you that she had died twelve months ago when her daughter had been taken from her. She was still breathing, still crying and still feeling pain. Apart from that, she did and felt nothing.

The pain was relentless. The medical diagnosis was clinical depression, but it all boiled down to pain. Mental anguish so intense that it caused her excruciating physical pain. Only relieved when she slept and she only slept when she had taken pills. And lots of them.

She had never liked sleeping pills. She felt like shit the next day and it was a high price to pay for chemically induced sleep. Always haunted by the same vivid nightmares.

Without the pills she didn't sleep at all. She'd just lie there staring at the ceiling, thinking of her daughter and crying. It was a vicious circle and she had decided to break it.

To end it.

She stood on the balcony of the fourth floor apartment at the Hotel Senator overlooking the sea at Marbella. It had been a nice idea to try to get away from it all, but it hadn't worked. The nightmares, the torment, had followed her and always would.

She had to end it now.

She had no idea where she had heard it but the phrase 'drop 'em long, stop 'em short' was going round and round in her head. Maybe it was that documentary about Albert Pierrepoint that she had seen on TV. She didn't know and she didn't care.

She checked the knot one last time. The rope was tied to the radiator as tight as she could get it. She fed the slack over the railings, put the loop in the other end over her head and pulled it tight. Then she climbed over the railings and stood with her back to the balcony holding on with her hands behind her. She thought about her daughter and the pain hit her as it always did. Like a sledgehammer.

This was not about being with her daughter. This was about putting an end to the pain. Tears began to stream down her cheeks.

Then she let go.

Chapter One

It had been a good day. All in all. The official report would record his involvement as 'drug squad liaison' but it ensured that Dixon had been first through Conrad Benton's front door when the battering ram had smashed it off its hinges. Benton obliged still further by taking a swing at Dixon. He ducked under the punch and then watched while two unusually large drug squad officers jumped on Benton and handcuffed him. Seldom had Dixon enjoyed arresting anyone more.

'Conrad Benton, I am arresting you on suspicion of assaulting a police officer. You do not have to say anything but it may harm your defence if you do not mention when questioned something that you later rely on in court. Anything you do say may be given in evidence.'

Benton did not reply.

The search of Benton's flat turned up PMA and ecstasy with a street value of over eight thousand pounds and, given his previous record, he could look forward to a lengthy spell in prison. Dixon arrested Benton again for the possession of class A drugs with intent to supply.

It had been an immensely satisfying morning's work.

Dixon had spent the afternoon on the beach with his dog, Monty, and then the evening with Detective Constable Jane Winter in the Zalshah Tandoori Restaurant in Burnham-on-Sea. He had eaten in a few curry houses in his time but had not found a better one than the Zalshah. He had not yet reached the point of being offered his 'usual' when he went in but he was already on first name terms with the waiters.

An added bonus was having managed to avoid telling Jane about his medal. She had forgotten about it and he had not reminded her.

Dixon watched the lights of passing cars flicker on the ceiling of his bedroom and allowed his mind to wander back to days on the sea cliffs at Pembroke, climbing in glorious sunshine with the waves crashing against the rocks beneath his feet.

The next thing he knew, his phone was ringing. He checked the time. 7.15 a.m.

'Nick Dixon.'

'Nick, it's DCI Lewis. Where are you?'

'In bed, Sir.'

'Whose?'

'Mine.'

'Where's Jane Winter? She's not answering her phone.'

'I think she said she was going to her parents' for the weekend. Why?'

'I need the pair of you over at Berrow Church as soon as you can.'

'I'm sure I can get hold of her, Sir.'

Dixon reached over and placed his left hand on Jane's right breast. She pulled the duvet over her head to stifle her laughter.

'Good. Get over there as quick as you can. They've found a severed head in one of the bunkers on the golf course.'

Dixon sat up sharply.

'A head? Where's the rest of the body?'

'We don't know yet. It's on the hole behind the church. The twelfth, I think it is.'

Dixon was already on his way to the bathroom.

'I'm on my way, Sir.'

Jane was dressed by the time Dixon emerged from the bathroom.

'Your parents live in Weston, don't they?'

'Yes. Well, Worle actually.'

'Give me twenty minutes' head start and then set off. Meet me at Berrow Church. That should be about right, shouldn't it?'

'I don't mind people knowing, if that's what's worrying you.'

'They'll know soon enough, Jane. When we're both good and ready.'

'Do you want me to feed Monty?'

'I'll take him with me, don't worry.'

Dixon had dressed in a hurry and was checking his pockets for his car keys.

'Help yourself to anything you want to eat and I'll see you at Berrow.'

Dixon left his cottage just before 7.30 a.m. It was well after sunrise and yet still almost dark. There was a heavy blanket of grey cloud, not a breath of wind, and a fine drizzle was falling as he drove out of Brent Knoll on the country roads towards Berrow.

He turned left into Station Road, presumably there had once been a railway station, and over the humpback bridge taking the road over the railway line. His mind went back, as it always did at this bridge, to an incident many years before, when he was only nine years old. His mother had been driving and they had been approaching the same bridge. For some reason, still unknown to her, his mother had pulled in and stopped just before the crest.

A split second later, a bus had careered over the bridge in the middle of the road. Both would certainly have been killed in a head on collision with the bus, had his mother not stopped. Such is the narrow margin between life and death.

He arrived in Berrow within two or three minutes and drove through the village slowly. He stopped at the Berrow Triangle and was pleased to see that the Berrow Inn was still open. They would be doing a roaring trade over the next few days with police officers, journalists and sightseers. He could also see that the Berrow Stores, scene of his one and only crime, was still open. He had stolen a packet of football stickers. It had turned out to be a complete waste of effort because he had got all of the footballers in the packet anyway.

He turned right onto Coast Road, heading towards Berrow Church. The drizzle was still falling and looked set for the day. He drove past the village green, past the roadside posters advertising the village fireworks display, and on towards the church.

Dixon's mind was racing. So many questions and all of them unanswered. The only thing that he could be reasonably sure of was that anyone throwing a severed head into a bunker on a golf course intended it to be found.

He turned into the Berrow Church car park. It was much as he had remembered it. The church stood on the edge of the sand dunes behind the Burnham and Berrow golf course. The entrance gates were new, as was the tarmac path leading to the front door, but the path beyond that was familiar to him. It was a narrow, sandy track in the grass leading up through the churchyard to a gap in the wall and out onto the golf course. The large yellow sign on the wall was also new: 'There is no lead on this church roof'. The Cross of St George fluttered from the flagpole on the top of the church tower.

Dixon noticed that the churchyard had been extended beyond the old wall, although looking at the dates on the headstones this could have been done some time ago, unless they had been moved. The car park had also been extended, although maybe he had just never noticed it before.

Dixon was greeted by PC Cole.

'I thought you were based at Cheddar?' asked Dixon.

'I am, Sir, but needs must at this time on a Sunday morning.'

Dixon put on his coat. Monty was raring to go.

'Not this time, matey. Later.'

Dixon turned to PC Cole.

'The twelfth, is it, then, Constable?'

'Greenside bunker on the twelfth, yes, Sir. Follow the path up through the churchyard, through the gap in the wall and then turn right. You will see PC Carroll.'

'Are Scenes of Crime on their way?'

'Yes, Sir.'

'Has anyone thought to cancel the church service? It is a Sunday morning, after all.'

'No, Sir.'

'Better ring the vicar, then. His telephone number is on the sign over there.'

'Will do, Sir.'

Dixon walked up the tarmac path to the entrance to the church and then continued along the sandy track. He noticed a line of small dark stains in the sand that had not been visible on the tarmac path. He immediately stepped sideways onto the grass and walked back down to the car park. PC Cole was on the telephone to the vicar breaking the news that the church service would need to be cancelled.

Once back onto the gravel car park, Dixon was able to pick up the trail of dark stains again. He followed it around to the right into the overflow car park. The trail ended by the bicycle rack. Dixon looked around. The area was well hidden from the road.

Dixon turned to PC Cole who had by now finished his telephone call. 'Cancelled?'

'Yes.'

'I want this area of the car park and the path through the churchyard cordoned off. There's a trail of what looks like blood that starts here and goes right up to the wall and possibly beyond. The scenes of crime team may be able to get something from tyre tracks or footprints.'

'Yes, Sir.'

'Send anyone else arriving around to the right.'

Dixon pointed to a track that led to a steel five bar gate and out onto the golf course.

'Tell them to turn left once through that gate and then left again up to the twelfth green.'

'Yes, Sir.'

Dixon walked back up through the churchyard making sure that he was clear of the tarmac path and the sandy track. Once through the wall the path forked. The main path turned sharp left, running along the back of the churchyard. There was a new fence in place that ran parallel to the stone wall until it joined the public right of way that led across the golf course to the beach. Dixon ignored this path and forked right. He followed the trail of blood through a gap in the fence. He could see the twelfth green off to his right and followed the path through the undergrowth to get to it. He arrived to find PC Carroll talking to a man wearing green overalls.

'Good morning, Constable. DI Dixon.'

'PC Carroll, Sir. Good morning. This is Michael Walker, one of the greenkeepers here. He found it.'

'Good morning, Mr Walker.'

Dixon stepped forward and looked into the bunker. He was immediately grateful that he had not had time for breakfast. He had never regarded himself as squeamish. It was not the sight of the blood that upset him, more the look on the person's face. The eyes were wide and bulging. The mouth was wide open and the tongue sticking out. The look was one of utter surprise, shock and horror all rolled into one. The victim had clearly known what was happening.

The bunker itself was one a golfer would describe as a deep pot bunker. It was situated at the back of the twelfth green and to the left as the hole was played. Dixon reckoned it was probably four feet deep.

He had lost the trail of blood in the long grass once out onto the golf course but had picked it up again at the edge of the bunker. There was a significant pool of blood at the right hand corner where the murderer had paused briefly before throwing the severed head in. A second and heavier trail of blood led across the golf course in the direction of the beach.

The head appeared to have struck the front face of the bunker and then rolled to the bottom. It was lying on its side facing Dixon. There was a large patch of dark bloodstained sand underneath it.

The head had been severed at shoulder level, giving the impression that the deceased had a very long neck. It appeared to be a clean cut. The victim was female with long grey hair, and Dixon estimated her age as between sixty-five and seventy-five years. But it was the look on her face that he knew would stay with him.

Dixon turned to PC Carroll.

'Scenes of Crime are on their way. I want this bunker sealed off and no one goes near it until they have arrived. Is that clear?'

'Yes, Sir.'

Dixon turned to the greenkeeper.

'When did you find it?'

'About an hour ago. I was out raking the bunkers for the monthly medal.'

'The monthly medal? Is there a golf competition this morning?'

'Yes.'

'What time does it start?'

'At 7.30 a.m.'

Dixon looked at his watch. It was just before 8 a.m.

'Ten minute intervals?'

'Yes.'

'That would be four groups out on the course and another just about to tee off. Has anyone rung the clubhouse to call it off?'

'You can't do that,' said Walker.

'It's not an option, I'm afraid. This is a crime scene and the course is closed.'

'I'd better get back to the clubhouse and let them know,' said Walker.

'You stay where you are, please, Mr Walker. We'll need a formal statement from you before you go.'

Dixon reached for his mobile phone and rang Jane.

'Where are you?'

'Coming along the Berrow Road.'

'I've got a job for you. Do you know the Burnham and Berrow Golf Club?'

'Yes. St Christopher's Way.'

'The monthly competition started at 7.30 a.m. and we need to stop it. The little building to the left of the clubhouse is the pro shop. Go in there and tell the pro, I can't remember his name, to call off the competition. OK?'

'I'm on my way.'

'They also need to send someone out onto the course in a buggy to call in those golfers who have already started.'

'Understood.'

'Anyone gives you any trouble, and I expect they will, you put them onto me.'

'I certainly will.'

Dixon rang off. He could hear PC Carroll's radio crackle into life.

'Scientific Services are here, Sir.'

Dixon walked back down to the car park, which was now a hive of activity. There were three police cars, an ambulance and two white vans signwritten 'Scientific Services Unit'. The overflow car park and the path up through the churchyard had been cordoned off with blue tape. PC Cole had at least got that right.

Dixon could see the senior scenes of crime officer, Donald Watson, directing one team to focus on the overflow car park and the path through the churchyard. Photographs were already being taken and it was still sufficiently dark for flashes to be required.

Watson walked over to Dixon.

'Where is it, then?'

Dixon pointed to the track leading off to the right.

'Follow that track through the five bar gate and then keep turning left. You can see the twelfth green in front of you. It's in the bunker at the back of the green.'

Dixon thought it odd that he had referred to the severed head as '*it*'. If it had been a body, male or female, then it would be 'he' or 'she'. The final indignity, perhaps, as if she had not suffered enough already.

Watson and the other team of scenes of crime officers set off towards the twelfth green.

Dixon gestured to PC Cole.

'Get the helicopter up with its thermal imaging camera, will you? Anyone gives you any trouble, you let me know.'

'What are they looking for, Sir?'

'Would you like me to draw you a diagram?'

'No, Sir.'

Dixon's mobile phone rang.

'What's up, Jane?'

'The club secretary's not happy. He's on his way to see you in a buggy.'

'Have they called off the competition?'

'Yes, but they're kicking up a hell of a stink. The acting chief constable is playing in it, apparently.'

'Not anymore he's not. Well done. Now get over here as quick as you can.'

Dixon walked back up to the green. The bunker was already covered by a large tent and Dixon could see camera flashes going off as he approached. He overheard PC Carroll talking to one of the scenes of crime officers.

'Give me a sand wedge and I'll get it out for you.'

'One more remark like that, Constable, and you're going to be in deep trouble. Show some respect.'

'Yes, Sir. Sorry, Sir.'

Dixon pointed to the line of bloodstains leading off towards the thirteenth fairway and the beach.

'Follow that trail and see where it goes.'

'Yes, Sir.'

Watson turned to Dixon.

'Odd place to hide a head, Nick?'

'Have a look around. What do you see?'

'Bushes.'

'Not just bushes. Dense undergrowth. If you wanted to hide a severed head, you'd throw it in there, wouldn't you? This wasn't hidden. It was left for us to find.'

Watson nodded and then disappeared inside the tent.

Dixon could hear the helicopter overhead. He turned to PC Cole, who had walked up to the green, and nodded towards the helicopter.

'Get them on the radio for me, will you?'

Dixon could see Jane walking up the twelfth fairway towards the green. He waved to her and she walked over to him.

'No sign of the secretary,' said Dixon.

'He was going to get the golfers off the course first.'

'Shame. I thought he'd changed his mind.'

Jane gestured towards the tent.

'Is it in there?'

'*It*' again, thought Dixon.

'Yes, but it's not a pretty sight.'

'Are you trying to protect me again?'

'Not at all, Jane. You're an investigating officer; you need to see it. I'd give the same warning to anyone at this time on a Sunday morning.'

'Good.'

'My guess is it's a woman aged between sixty-five and seventy-five. See what you think.'

PC Cole interrupted.

'Helicopter's on the radio, Sir.'

He passed the radio to Dixon.

'We've got a severed head in the bunker. That means there must be a body somewhere. There may be some heat left in it, so see if you can see anything with your thermal imaging camera. OK? Check the beach too.'

'Roger that, will do.'

Dixon hated 'radiospeak'. He watched the helicopter move off towards the far end of the golf course. Unfortunately, he then noticed a golf buggy driving towards him. Instinctively, he straightened his tie as he walked around the twelfth green and down the fairway towards the buggy, intending to intercept it.

The buggy screeched to a halt in front of him.

'I'm looking for Detective Inspector Dixon.'

'Yes.'

'My name is Paul Durkin. I'm the club secretary. We've had to postpone the start of our competition and I've got over a hundred golfers waiting to tee off.'

'Cancel is a more accurate description, I'm afraid, Mr Durkin. The course is closed.'

'Closed?'

'Yes, and it's likely to remain so for at least the rest of today.'

'The acting chief constable will have something to say about this. He's teeing off at 10.30.'

'I can assure you that he will have even more to say about it if I don't close the course. Can I suggest, therefore, that someone telephones any golfer who has not already arrived at the course, and it might also be sensible to send the others home.'

'This is a disgrace. What on earth can have happened?'

'You will appreciate that I cannot be too specific at the present time. Suffice it to say that a murder has been committed and the bunker you can see up there is a crime scene.'

'Oh, my God. Is the body in there?'

'I really can't say, but I would be grateful if you would cancel the competition and send everyone home immediately.'

'Yes, I will. I will. Constable Winter never said it was a murder.'

He looked white as a sheet as he climbed into his buggy and followed the track down towards the thirteenth tee.

Dixon walked back up to the green to meet Jane, who was surprisingly unscathed by her experience in the tent.

'You must have a stronger stomach than me,' said Dixon.

Jane smiled.

'Did you lose your breakfast?' she asked.

'I would have done if I'd had any.'

Dixon pointed to Michael Walker.

'Jane, that's the greenkeeper. He found it this morning. Get a detailed statement from him, will you? Usual drill. You can sit in the church. It's open, I think.'

'Will do.'

PC Cole shouted across to Dixon.

'DCI Lewis has arrived, Sir. He's on his way up.'

Dixon turned to Jane.

'That's all we need!'

Dixon could see DCI Lewis walking up the twelfth fairway towards the green. He turned to PC Cole.

'Find out where the pathologist is, will you? He should be here by now.'

'Yes, Sir.'

Dixon met DCI Lewis on the edge of the green.

'What have we got, then, Nick?'

'A severed head in the bunker, Sir. Pathologist is on his way and I've got the helicopter up with its thermal imaging camera looking for the rest of the body.'

'Good.'

'There's a trail of blood leading across the golf course towards the beach so it's possible the murderer carried the head across the golf course. There's a pool of blood at the edge of the bunker where he or she paused before throwing it in.'

Lewis nodded.

'A smaller trail then leads down to the overflow car park so I'm thinking the murderer left his car there.'

'Anyone checking the beach?'

'I've asked the helicopter to have a look and I've got a constable following the trail to see where it goes.'

'Good.'

'It looks to me to be a female aged between sixty-five and seventy-five but I will wait for Dr Poland to confirm that. I've cancelled the church service and also called off the golf competition that had started.'

'I bet that went down well.'

'It caused a bit of a rumpus. Apparently, the acting chief con was playing in it.'

'You'll be popular.'

PC Cole interrupted.

'The vicar is here, Sir, wondering whether he can be of any assistance.'

'Tell him I'll pop down for a chat with him in a minute.'

Dixon turned back to DCI Lewis.

'It's not a pretty sight, I'm afraid, Sir.'

'Don't worry, Nick, I'm used to it.'

Dixon dropped back down to the church car park to meet the vicar, who introduced himself as the Reverend Stephen Bessent. Dixon thanked him for his concern and politely explained, without being too specific, that he could not be of assistance on this occasion. He explained that the vicar would be unlikely to recognise the victim, even if he or she had been a member of his congregation. The vicar confirmed that he had not had reports of anyone missing. He asked whether he would also need to cancel evensong at 6 p.m. and Dixon confirmed that he would.

Dixon turned to see Dr Roger Poland, senior pathologist at Musgrove Park Hospital, turning into the car park. They had first met only a few weeks before on the South Drain at Gold Corner Pumping Station when Dr Poland had suggested getting together for a drink. Dr Poland parked his car and walked across to greet Dixon.

'Hello, Nick. I gather you had a bit of a close shave at the Clarence.'

'Let's just say it was interesting.'

'Enough said. What have we got here?'

'A severed head in the bunker at the back of the twelfth green. Looks to me like an elderly woman. No one has been in the bunker yet, so it's over to you.'

'Jolly good, lead on.'

Dixon walked back up to the green with Dr Poland, who disappeared inside the tent to begin his examination of the severed head. This would, of course, involve setting foot in the sand, but scenes of crime officers would by now have finished their forensic examination and photographing of the bunker. Dixon decided to leave Dr Poland to it.

Dr Poland reappeared five minutes later.

'I've finished my preliminary examination. You're right, it's an elderly white female approximately seventy years of age. It's a clean cut at shoulder level, possibly using some sort of electric blade, and there are what appear to be ligature marks further up the neck. My guess, and it is only a guess at this stage, is that she was already dead before she was decapitated.'

'Already dead?' asked Dixon.

'Yes, but I'll need the rest of the body to confirm.'

'Any idea how long?'

'Last night or the early hours of this morning. If the helicopter is up looking for a heat trace they're wasting their time.'

Dixon turned to PC Cole.

'Tell the helicopter they can go home, please, Constable. Ask them to check the beach first.'

'Well, unless there's anything else, I really need to get the head back to the hospital,' said Poland.

'Yes, that's fine.'

Two mortuary technicians in white overalls appeared carrying what looked to Dixon to be a large black picnic box.

DCI Lewis had emerged from the tent and had been listening in.

'Is there anything else you need, Nick?'

'A few more officers so we can start a house to house in the local area, please, Sir. It might also be worth getting a sniffer dog to follow that trail and see where it goes.'

'Good thinking. I'll organise that straight away and see you back at Bridgwater later.'

'Yes, Sir, thank you.'

Dixon watched while the mortuary technicians emerged from the tent with *it* in the black picnic box. He took some comfort from the fact that her suffering, and she clearly had suffered, was over. He had never been religious but was grateful for the closeness of the church at that particular moment.

Dixon turned to see Jane running up the fairway towards him. She arrived more than a little out of breath.

'We're getting reports of a burnt out car on the beach and there's a body in the driver's seat. A headless body. It's near the old shipwreck.'

'Has Dr Poland left yet?'

'No. Nor has DCI Lewis.'

Dixon and Jane raced down to the car park. Dr Poland and DCI Lewis were ready to go, so Dixon and Jane jumped into Jane's car and headed for the beach, with Dr Poland and DCI Lewis following in their own cars. They drove out of the church car park, turned left along Coast Road and continued until they saw the left turn for Berrow Beach. They were greeted at the entrance by a police constable who removed the blue tape, allowing the convoy of vehicles through. The solid five bar steel gates at the entrance to the beach were permanently open this time of year. They were only closed during the summer months, enabling the council to charge four pounds for the privilege of parking on the beach.

They drove out along the tarmac road heading straight towards the beach, past the Sundowner Café, through the dunes and out onto the Berrow flats. The tide was out, revealing a huge expanse of sand. Dixon could see Brean Down to the north and Hinkley Point power station across the estuary.

Another police constable on the beach gestured to the south. Jane turned left and headed along the beach towards a vehicle they could see parked in the distance.

'Back towards the golf course,' said Dixon.

They arrived to find the remains of what looked like a red Fiat Uno. It was parked facing out to sea, just inland from the wreck of the SS *Nornen*. The tide was out and the skeletal remains of the old ship protruded from the sand. The timbers reached skyward and reminded Dixon of the ribs on a rotting carcass.

Dixon looked inland. No more than fifty yards away was a path leading across the golf course through a gap in the sand dunes.

'Get someone to follow that path, Jane. They should meet PC Carroll coming the other way.'

'Where does it go?'

'Straight across the course to the church.'

Dixon got out of Jane's car and walked around the Fiat Uno. The passenger compartment had been almost entirely destroyed by fire, leaving the engine intact. Clearly, this was not an engine fire that got out of control. He noticed that the rear number plate was still there. Saved by the rain, no doubt. They would be able to trace the vehicle and, hopefully, identify the owner, if someone had not already done so.

He could also see a charred body in the driver's seat. It was leaning forward, resting against the steering wheel and its head was missing.

It again.

Dixon opened the passenger door of Jane's car and leaned in.

'Get Watson and his team over here as quick as you can. We're in a race with the tide now so this must be the priority.'

'Yes, Sir.'

'Tell them not to worry too much about tyre tracks.'

'Why not?'

'Washed away on this morning's tide. Look.'

Dixon watched DCI Lewis parking behind Jane. Then he leaned back into Jane's car through the open door.

'And find out what time high tide is.'

'OK.'

He turned to DCI Lewis, who spoke first.

'We're going to have the press all over this any minute now. I'll get onto the press officer. She can organise liaison. The buggers are going to have a field day.'

'Don't they always?'

'We'll sort out the details of exactly what we release later. OK?'

'Yes, Sir.'

Dixon approached the police constable standing by the burnt out car.

'And you are?'

'WPC Willmott, Sir.'

'Who found it?'

'A Mrs Diane Weller. She was out walking her dog. I've got her address.'

'You let her go?'

'Yes, Sir. She was very distressed, I'm afraid. She lives locally, though, and will be available to speak to you when required.'

'Have you checked the number plate?'

'Yes.'

WPC Willmott produced her notebook.

'The registered keeper is a Valerie Manning of 7 Manor Drive, Berrow.'

'That's right opposite the church, isn't it?'

'Yes, Sir. Just off Manor Way.'

Dixon turned to Jane.

'You know what to do, Jane.'

'Yes, Sir.'

Jane went back to her car, sat in the driver's seat and reached for her radio.

Dixon addressed WPC Willmott again.

'We'll need a flatbed lorry to recover this vehicle when the pathologist has finished, Constable. Can you rustle that up, please?'

'Yes, Sir.'

'Otherwise, it's over to you, Roger.'

Roger Poland was looking in through the driver's side window of the Fiat Uno.

'The body is badly burned, I'm afraid, and there's a strong smell of petrol. I can see what looks like a stab wound below the left shoulder blade. Subject to its depth, that would have been sufficient to kill her. I won't really know though until I do the post mortem. I'll get that done as quick as I can.'

'Thanks, Roger. I'll leave you to it.'

DCI Lewis shouted across to Dixon.

'I've spoken to the press officer. She's had journalists on already so she's going to go for a press conference at 6 p.m. today, OK?'

'If we must, Sir.'

'And Dave Harding and Mark Pearce are on their way to give you a hand.'

'Thank you.'

DCI Lewis gave Dixon a wave, got back into his car and drove back down the beach. Dixon got into the passenger seat of Jane's car.

'Well?'

'Valerie Manning. Sixty-eight years of age. Married to Peter. Lives at 7 Manor Drive. The electoral roll shows possibly one adult son still living at home. None of them are known to police.'

'Right. Well, we've got Dave Harding and Mark Pearce coming, so we'll wait until they get here and then go and knock on the door and see what we find.'

'OK.'

'See if you can get a family liaison officer out here as well, just in case.'

Jane nodded and reached for her radio.

'God alone knows how we're going to deal with the identification,' said Dixon.

Chapter Two

By mid-afternoon the forensic examination of each scene was largely complete. The burnt out Fiat Uno had been recovered from the beach just before the high tide reached it and the sand had been dug out of the bunker on the twelfth hole. A fingertip search of the church car park and the path across the golf course was now under way but it would be dark soon and so this was likely to go into a second day. House to house enquiries were also taking place in the local area, with the exception of Manor Drive.

Valerie Manning was now in the mortuary at Musgrove Park Hospital, awaiting her post mortem. Dixon was not sure whether her head had been reunited with her body or her body reunited with her head but, either way, it would not be long before she could rest in peace.

The golf club secretary, Paul Durkin, had recovered his composure and was suitably outraged at the likely closure of the course for a second day. He was equally concerned by the removal of the sand from the bunker, which would have to be designated 'ground under repair' until it could be replaced. Dixon could not understand the fuss, given that there was no shortage of sand in the vicinity.

He had managed to fit in a brief lunch sitting in his Land Rover with Monty, followed by a short walk on the beach. He was now waiting for the family liaison officer to arrive before knocking on the door of 7 Manor Drive. House to house enquiries at the other properties in Manor Drive would start at the same time.

———

The family liaison officer arrived shortly before 4 p.m. Police Sergeant Karen Marsden was in her early forties with bleached blonde hair. She wore dark trousers and a cream top under a navy blue jacket. Dixon thought it unusual to see a police sergeant out of uniform but the work of family liaison no doubt required a less formal approach.

They knocked on the door of 7 Manor Drive just after 4 p.m. It was a large red brick house with a built in double garage. Dixon was relieved that Karen Marsden had agreed to do the talking, at least initially, but no doubt there would come a point when he would need to ask the difficult questions. The door was answered by a large man in his early seventies. He was balding and wore dark horn rimmed spectacles. He was dressed casually and wore an open neck shirt, cardigan and dark corduroys. Karen Marsden spoke first.

'We are looking for Mr Peter Manning.'

'Yes.'

He looked suspicious but then so would anyone confronted with three people on their doorstep at four o'clock on a Sunday afternoon. Dixon thought he could read nothing into that.

'I am Police Sergeant Karen Marsden. This is Detective Inspector Nick Dixon and Detective Constable Jane Winter. We'd like to have a word with you, if we may, Mr Manning.'

'It's not Simon, is it?'

'No, Sir. May we come in?'

'Yes, of course.'

Peter Manning stepped to one side allowing Karen Marsden, Jane and then Dixon into his hallway. Dixon looked to his right before he went in and could see the other properties in Manor Drive being called upon by police officers conducting house to house enquiries.

'Go through into the sitting room,' said Peter Manning, gesturing towards an open door adjacent to the foot of the stairs.

'Please sit down.'

Karen Marsden and Jane sat on a sofa opposite the fireplace. Dixon sat in the armchair to their right. Peter Manning stood with his back to the fire. He turned to Dixon.

'May I see your warrant cards again? I didn't get a clear look at them on the doorstep.'

'Certainly,' said Dixon, producing his warrant card from his inside jacket pocket. Karen Marsden and Jane produced their warrant cards from their handbags and handed them to Peter Manning. He looked at them carefully and then handed them back.

'How can I help?'

'When did you last see your wife, Mr Manning?' asked Karen Marsden.

'Yesterday. She went to the theatre in Bristol with some friends.'

'And you've not seen her since?'

'No.'

'Do you have a photograph of her?'

'Yes, of course.' Manning turned around and took a photograph off the mantelpiece. He passed it to Karen Marsden, who looked at it and then passed it to Dixon. It was a photograph of Valerie Manning holding a Yorkshire terrier. He glanced across at Jane and nodded before handing the photograph back to Karen Marsden.

'Is it unusual for Mrs Manning to stay out all night?' Karen Marsden continued.

'No, not unusual. Why, is there a problem?'

'Is anyone else living here with you?'

'Our eldest son is, temporarily. He's getting divorced, unfortunately.'

'Is that Simon?'

'Yes.'

'Is he in at the moment?'

'No, he's taken his children out for the day. He only gets to see them every couple of weeks.'

'Is there anyone else you can ring, who can come and sit with you?'

'You are starting to worry me now. There's my daughter and son-in-law. They live at Edithmead.'

'Could you give them a ring and get them to come over?'

'Yes, yes, of course. What's happened to Val, for God's sake?'

'I am sorry to have to tell you, Mr Manning, but we have found a body and have reason to believe that it's your wife,' said Karen Marsden.

'Found a body? You mean she's dead?'

'Yes, I'm afraid that she is.'

Dixon had long since given up trying to interpret how people reacted when informed that a loved one had died. He invariably arrived at a different conclusion to his colleagues, and people reacted in so many disparate ways. Having said that, it was the first occasion that Dixon could recall the news that a man's wife had died being greeted with a wry smile and shrug of the shoulders. Dixon looked at Jane and then Karen Marsden. Clearly, they too had found Manning's reaction odd.

Karen Marsden handed the photograph back to Peter Manning. He looked at it, sat on a chair next to the telephone table in the front window of 7 Manor Drive, put his head in his hands and began to sob. It was several minutes before he regained his composure. Dixon took the initiative.

'I'm a bit confused, Mr Manning . . .'

Manning wiped the tears from his eyes.

'Perhaps I should explain. Val and I haven't enjoyed a good relationship for some time. We should have gone our separate ways long ago, but we can't sell this fucking house, thanks to the recession. Nothing's selling, At least, not at a sensible price. So, we are stuck here. Trapped together, you might say.'

'And the tears?'

'For old times' sake. We were close once.'

'So, you lead separate lives?'

'Entirely separate.'

'Have you started divorce proceedings?'

'She served me with a divorce petition but we haven't got the Decree Absolute yet.'

'It must be difficult, living under the same roof.'

'It was. We've got used to it now. Resigned to it is probably a better word. Now, we can just about tolerate each other.'

'Where were you last night between 11 p.m. and 2 a.m.?'

'Here with Simon. Hang on a minute, what the hell has happened?'

'Mr Manning, I'm sorry to have to tell you that your wife has been murdered.'

'Murdered?'

'Yes. We are going to need a detailed account of your movements last night. We are also going to need to speak to Simon. Do you have his mobile number?'

'Yes, of course. He's with his sons, though.'

Jane made a note of Simon Manning's mobile number and then left the room to speak to him. Karen Marsden used the opportunity to make some tea. When they were left alone, Peter Manning turned to Dixon.

'How did she die?'

'We're not sure yet, I'm afraid. The post mortem is due later today or possibly tomorrow morning, but at this stage it looks as though she was stabbed.'

'Did she suffer?'

'No.' Dixon lied.

'Am I a suspect?'

'You'd have to admit you have just given us a powerful motive.'

'I suppose I have, but I didn't kill her.'

Jane appeared in the doorway.

'Simon is on his way back from Bristol Zoo. I've arranged for Dave and Mark to meet him at his ex-wife's house.'

'Good, Jane. Thank you.'

Karen Marsden reappeared with tea for all.

'Shall I ring my daughter now?' asked Manning.

'Not yet. We are going to need a detailed statement from you, Mr Manning, if you wouldn't mind coming with us to the station,' replied Dixon.

'Not at all. I want to help. I've got nothing to hide.'

'In that case, would you also be content for us to search the house?'

'I'm sure you don't need my permission.'

'No, as it happens, we don't.'

———

Usually closed at the weekend, Burnham-on-Sea Police Station was now the incident room for the investigation. This meant that Karen Marsden and Jane would be able to use the interview suite there to take a statement from Peter Manning rather than travel all the way to Bridgwater. Dixon reminded Jane that Peter Manning was not under arrest. He was a bereaved relative assisting police with their enquiries and was to be afforded every courtesy unless and until they had evidence to the contrary. A shrug of the shoulders at the news of his wife's death and ongoing divorce proceedings were not themselves evidence of murder.

Dixon returned to Bridgwater Police Station for a meeting with DCI Lewis and the press officer. The press conference was due at 6 p.m. He had not previously met the press officer, every effort having been made to keep his last case out of the newspapers.

It was very rare that Dixon took an instant dislike to someone. He would usually wait until they had given him good reason to dislike them. It had only happened on perhaps two or three occasions previously and his initial judgement had always proved correct. Before DCI Lewis had introduced them, Dixon decided that he did not like the press officer, although it was unclear to him why he had arrived at that conclusion. She was in her late forties, with long, straight blonde hair and sharp features. She wore a pinstriped skirt and jacket with a white blouse.

DCI Lewis made the introductions.

'Thankfully, we managed to keep your last fiasco out of the papers,' said Vicky Thomas.

'I can see that you and I are going to get on like a house on fire,' replied Dixon.

DCI Lewis intervened.

'Let's focus on the job in hand, shall we? What can we tell them?'

'We can tell them that the victim had been decapitated, I think. It's inevitable that will leak from the golf club. Otherwise, there has been no formal identification, although the family have been informed,' replied Dixon.

'Anything else?' asked Lewis.

'The murder took place sometime between 11 p.m. last night and 2 a.m. this morning. The charred remains of her body were found by a dog walker in a burnt out car on the beach at Berrow and her head was found by a member of the greens staff in a bunker on the Burnham and Berrow golf course.'

Both Lewis and Vicky Thomas were taking notes. Dixon continued.

'And that the victim is an elderly white female, aged approximately seventy. A detailed search of the scene will be going into a second day and house to house enquiries are continuing.'

'Haven't you got the husband in custody?' asked Vicky Thomas.

'News travels fast. No. He's not under arrest. He's helping us with our enquiries at this stage and I certainly don't think we should be releasing any information that may identify the family.'

'Agreed,' said DCI Lewis. 'We don't want a repeat of that shambles in Bristol.'

Dixon glanced across at Vicky Thomas. She was looking at her shoes.

'Lastly, an appeal for information,' said Dixon. 'Anyone who saw anything unusual in the vicinity of Berrow Church, the beach and on Coast Road on Saturday or the early hours of Sunday morning to contact the incident room, etc., etc.'

DCI Lewis turned to Dixon.

'Are you going to sit in?'

'Yes, Sir, if I must.'

'I think it would be a good idea,' said Vicky Thomas.

Dixon's phone was ringing in his pocket. He looked at the caller ID.

'I'd better take this,' he said, getting up and leaving the room.

'Hello, Roger.'

'Nick, I'm just about to start the PM. Can you get here? It's going to be a very interesting one, I think.'

'Yes, I'm on my way.'

'Do you know where we are?'

'Yes.'

'Park next to my car. You won't get a ticket on a Sunday. You'll see the green doors. Just ring the bell and someone will come and get you.'

'I'll be with you in twenty minutes. And thanks, Roger. Perfect timing.'

Dixon stood in the doorway of DCI Lewis' office.

'That was Roger Poland. He's about to start the PM and thinks it would be a good idea if I was there.'

'Convenient,' said Vicky Thomas.

'Very. I'll see you tomorrow, Sir,' said Dixon, addressing DCI Lewis.

The post mortem was well under way by the time Dixon arrived at Musgrove Park Hospital. He had driven slowly in the hope that Dr Poland would start without him and his plan appeared to have worked. He had rung the bell and been let in by one of the technicians he had seen earlier carrying the black picnic box. He was shown through to an anteroom adjacent to the pathology lab and could see through viewing windows that Roger Poland was hard at work, Dictaphone in hand. He could see Valerie Manning laid out on the slab.

Dixon watched the mortuary technician go through into the laboratory and speak to Dr Poland. The next thing he knew, the intercom crackled into life.

'Don't just sit there. Come in. You won't see anything from there.'

Dixon was grateful that he had not had much to eat all day. Monty had eaten half his sandwich at lunchtime and he had kept himself going since then with medicinal fruit pastilles. Being diabetic was a pain at the best of times, but keeping his blood sugar levels up on days when he had no time to eat was always difficult. Fortunately, they were few and far between. Today it was a positive advantage. He took a deep breath and walked through into the lab.

'What have you got, then, Roger?' asked Dixon.

'Quite a lot, actually,' replied Poland. 'Take a look at this for starters.'

Poland pointed to Valerie Manning's neck. Dixon stepped forward. The sight that greeted him took his breath away. He stopped, closed his eyes and took a deep breath.

'Sick, is it?' asked Poland.

'Sickened,' replied Dixon.

Valerie Manning's eyes and mouth were now closed, affording her a measure of tranquility. Her head had been placed on the slab in its proper position on her body and she looked almost human again. Her charred and blackened body made a stark contrast to her white head and neck. Her lower legs and feet were also white and had clearly escaped the flames. She did at least appear at peace, and Dixon was grateful that he could now refer to her as '*she*' rather than '*it*'. He quickly regained his composure.

'What am I looking at?'

Then the smell hit him. Burnt flesh and petrol. He turned away sharply and walked over to the window. It was closed.

'Tracey, get Inspector Dixon a mask, will you?'

'Just give me a minute. I'll be fine.'

'Well, at least you didn't pass out.'

The mortuary technician handed Dixon a paper mask. He put it across his nose and mouth and hooked the elastic over his ears.

'There you go, you'll be OK now,' said Poland.

'Right then, let's try again, shall we?' said Dixon. 'What am I looking at?'

'The bruising on the neck. See it?'

'Yes.'

'A ligature of some sort. What sticks out is that it's uniform in width. See that? My guess is a belt was used.'

Dixon nodded.

'Look at this too.'

Poland stood at the end of the slab. He placed his hands either side of Valerie Manning's head and turned it to the left. Dixon was standing to Dr Poland's right. He looked away just in time.

'See? There's no bruising at the back of the neck.'

'I see that, yes.'

'It stops at the same point on either side. Have a look this side.'

Dixon walked around the back of Dr Poland while he turned Valerie Manning's head to the right.

'It does,' said Dixon.

'What does that tell you?' asked Poland.

'That the belt was used to tie her to something.'

'That's right. And we should be able to tell the width of whatever it was she was tied to by measuring the marks on her neck. It's basic trigonometry, really.'

'My money's on the headrest in her car.'

'That's your department,' said Poland.

'What about the cause of death?' asked Dixon.

'There are two wounds, both of which would have killed her.'

'Two?'

'Yes. There's the stab wound just below her left shoulder blade that penetrated her heart. A long thin blade, fish filleting knife or something like that.'

'And?'

'Her throat was cut.'

'Before her head was severed?'

'Yes, and using a different implement. That's how I can tell.'

'Show me,' said Dixon.

'I won't ask you to look too closely. The head was severed using an electric blade. The cuts are uniform in their stroke and that could only have been done with some form of electric carving knife. In places, though, there's a cut with no backwards and forwards stroke

31

to it. It's just a smooth sweep in one direction. That would have been made when her throat was cut. I can tell you her killer is right handed from that too.'

Dixon was making notes. 'Would an electric carving knife be powerful enough?' he asked.

'A top of the range one would be, or a fish filleting knife possibly. They're pretty powerful these days. It'll all be in my report,' said Poland. 'There's also a wound to the back of her left hand. Much of the flesh has been burnt away but it's still visible. A cut or slash. Something like that.'

'So, what actually killed her?' asked Dixon.

'The stab wound to the heart. From the blood loss, her throat was cut first. She was then stabbed in the back for good measure.'

'Why do you think the first cut was made so low on her neck? She's been decapitated almost at shoulder level, which is unusual, wouldn't you say?'

'That's easy, Nick. The belt was still around her neck at the time, so her throat was cut below it. Her head was then severed using the same incision. Make sense?'

'It does,' replied Dixon. 'And you think it's an electric carving knife?'

'Yes, something like that. Definitely not a chainsaw. You can tell them a mile away.'

'So, she's in the driver's seat of a four door Fiat Uno. Her killer is already sitting in or jumps into the back seat behind her. A belt is put around her neck, tying her to the headrest.'

'Very possible, yes,' said Poland.

'She's then forced to drive out to Berrow Beach where her throat is cut below the restraining belt. She's then stabbed in the back, for good measure, as you put it.'

Dixon paused.

'It would be interesting to know if she was stabbed through the car seat, Roger.'

'I can look for fibres when I open her up.'

'I'll get the forensic team to look for any marks on the seat too. The cover has been burnt away but there may be a mark on the frame,' said Dixon.

'All sounds good to me,' said Poland.

'Then the restraint is removed and her head severed. The car is then torched.'

'That certainly fits with what I've found so far. I've still got a few hours' work ahead of me, though.'

'And the wound on the back of her hand could have been inflicted either when she was taken or during the drive to the beach?'

'It could.'

'I'll leave you to it, then, Roger, if you don't mind,' said Dixon, removing his mask. 'We must have that beer sometime too.'

'That would be good, Nick,' replied Poland.

Dixon called in at Berrow Church to find the area still sealed off, with a panda car in attendance. He arrived home just after 8.30 p.m., fed Monty and sent text messages to Dave Harding and Mark Pearce, calling a briefing at Burnham-on-Sea Police Station for 8 a.m. the following day. He then sent a text message to Jane, asking where she was.

He felt sure that he heard the telltale 'bleep bleep' of a text message arriving. Seconds later there was a knock at his door. It was Jane. She held up a large white carrier bag full of silver trays.

'Chinese?'

'You, Jane, are a mind reader.'

Chapter Three

Dixon left home at 7.15 a.m. and called at Berrow Church on his way to Burnham-on-Sea Police Station. The fingertip search of the churchyard and golf course was due to start again at 8 a.m. He spoke to Police Sergeant Dean, who was coordinating the search.

'How many men have you got, Sergeant?'

'Thirty, Sir.'

'Dogs?'

'Yes, Sir.'

'Good. Check the undergrowth between the church and the green, will you? And around the car park.'

'What are we looking for, Sir?'

'Weapons, obviously. A knife and possibly also an electric carving knife or similar. Also a belt and a bag of some sort. Her head must have been carried here in something.'

'Yes, Sir.'

'Let me know when you've finished and I'll let the golf club know.'

'Yes, Sir.'

'And ring me immediately if you find anything.'

Dixon arrived at Burnham-on-Sea Police Station just before 8 a.m. It was a red brick building on the Burnham Road, midway between Burnham and Highbridge. Jane, Dave Harding and Mark Pearce were already there. As was DCI Lewis. Dixon wondered how he knew.

'Let's get on with it, then, shall we?' said Dixon.

The incident room was the old CID room on the second floor of the police station. It was used primarily for storage now that there was no permanent CID presence in Burnham, although some effort had been made to clear it for the current investigation. There was a whiteboard, and computers had been put in the afternoon before too.

Dixon pinned an enlarged version of the photograph of Valerie Manning holding the Yorkshire terrier on the whiteboard.

'This is our victim. Mrs Valerie Manning. Aged sixty-eight. Lives at 7 Manor Drive, Berrow with her husband, Peter, and son, Simon. Dinner lady at Berrow School. The formal identification will take place later today. The son's agreed to do it, hasn't he, Dave?'

'Yes, Sir.'

'Good. Married in name only, as we know. More on that in a minute. It's all over the press now and the nationals have picked it up too. It's out there that she was decapitated but nothing else. Let's keep it that way, please.'

All agreed.

'Right then, who spoke to Diane Weller, the lady who found the car?'

'We did,' said Dave Harding.

'Anything?' asked Dixon.

'No, not really. She was out with her dog, as usual apparently, saw the car in the distance and walked over to it. The tide was in round the wheels, which attracted her attention. When she had finished screaming she dialled 999. She was in a bit of a state, to be fair to her. She saw no one, heard nothing. There were no footprints or tyre tracks in the sand either. The tide was on its way out at the time.'

'Is that it?'

'She gave a statement but that's the gist of it, yes, Sir.'

'What about the greenkeeper, Jane?'

'Much the same. Saw nothing. Heard nothing. He was out raking the bunkers and found her head. Simple as that, really.'

'Ok, what about the husband, Jane?' asked Dixon. 'What did he have to say for himself?'

'He was quite open about their situation, I think. He admitted that the marriage was over and that they were trapped in the house because they couldn't sell it. Not at a sensible price anyway. It had been very difficult at first, when divorce proceedings started, but things had calmed down recently.'

'What does "very difficult" mean, I wonder?' asked Dixon.

'He admitted hitting her on a couple of occasions. Her solicitor applied for an injunction against him at one stage too. That was a while ago though.'

'We'd better have a word with her solicitor,' said Dixon.

'I've got her details,' said Jane.

'What about his alibi? Dave, you spoke to the son.'

'Holds up. At home all evening, apparently, watching the golf. It was the HSBC Champions, whatever that is. They both sat up and watched it until it finished at around midnight and then he went to bed. The son stayed up to watch a film and went to bed at about 2.30 a.m.'

'She was killed sometime between 11 p.m. and 2 a.m. so it's possible if the husband had gone out after midnight . . .'

'The son was adamant he would have heard his father go out, Sir, and says that he didn't,' said Mark Pearce.

'OK, we'll take that at face value for the time being. I don't think the husband did it, anyway,' said Dixon.

'Neither do I,' said Jane. 'Even though his reaction to the news of her death was a bit . . . odd.'

'So, her movements on Saturday night,' said Dixon. 'She went to the theatre in Bristol with two friends. We need detailed statements from those friends. I expect they met somewhere and went in one car. Where did they meet? I'm guessing that Valerie Manning left her car in a car park somewhere or perhaps outside a friend's house. CCTV will be crucial. We also need to look at every single traffic camera on their route between the end of the show and 2 a.m. Dave and Mark, that's your job. OK?'

'Yes, Sir,' in unison.

Dixon turned to DCI Lewis.

'They'll need some help with that, Sir, and we need some help with answering the phones.'

'Leave it to me.'

'Sometime between leaving her car and getting back into it at the end of the evening, someone got into the back seat and lay in wait for her. Or . . .' Dixon paused, '. . . they jumped her when she got back to her car. They could also have got into the back of the car when she was on her way home. While she was at traffic lights, perhaps, but this is less likely. Depending on her route, we may get a look at this person on one or more of the cameras. Better still there may be CCTV of the car park itself.'

'Do we know what happened then, Sir?' asked Pearce.

'We do. Some of this is guesswork and I am waiting for Dr Poland's final report but it looks as though a belt was used to tie her round the neck to the headrest of the car. She was then forced at knifepoint to drive to Berrow Beach. There's a superficial injury to the back of her left hand that may have been caused either when she was taken or during the drive to the beach.'

'Superficial?' asked Pearce.

'Compared to being decapitated, yes. Once on the beach, the killer slit her throat and then stabbed her through the heart. That was the fatal wound. It was a thin blade, possibly a fish filleting knife, and I expect we will find that she was stabbed through the car seat. That's to be confirmed.'

'Who the fuck would want to do that to a school dinner lady?' asked Pearce.

'Could she not have met the killer on the beach, Sir?' asked Harding.

'Possible but unlikely. Why else the neck restraint? According to Dr Poland, the belt was round her neck for some time. If the killer had met her on the beach, she would have been stabbed straight away, surely?'

'I suppose so.'

'We'll know soon enough, though,' Dixon continued. 'The belt was then untied from around her neck and she was decapitated using an electric carving knife or saw of some sort. Not a chainsaw. Dr Poland is quite definite about that. Her head was then taken, possibly in a bag, and the car set fire to.'

'We need to find that belt and bag,' said DCI Lewis.

'We do, Sir,' replied Dixon. 'As well as the knives. I briefed the search team this morning on my way here.'

'Good.'

'The killer then cut across the golf course, dumped her head in the bunker and left the scene in his car, which had been left in the church car park, hidden from view. That last bit is supposition, of course.'

'Sounds plausible,' said Lewis.

'Right then, let's get on with it. Jane, we need to speak to her solicitor and her sisters as well. She has two, I think. See if the family liaison officer can set that up. We'll pay a visit to Berrow School too. Meet back here at 6 p.m.'

'There's something about sitting outside a head teacher's office that just makes you feel guilty, isn't there?' whispered Dixon.

Jane rolled her eyes.

They had arrived at Berrow Primary School just after 9 a.m. and were now waiting outside the office of the head teacher, Ruth Smith. She was currently dealing with a set of parents and raised voices told Dixon that their child was not top of the class. The meeting ended abruptly. The door to Ruth Smith's office flew open and a young couple made for the exit at the far end of the corridor, closely followed by the head teacher. She turned to look at Dixon and Jane.

'And you are?'

'Detective Inspector Dixon and Detective Constable Winter. Avon and Somerset Police,' replied Dixon, producing his warrant card. Jane did the same.

Ruth Smith was in her early fifties, slim, with short greying hair. She wore black trousers and a purple blouse.

'Oh, yes, of course. Come in. Sorry about that. Nobody likes being told their child is a bully, do they?'

'No,' said Dixon.

'Do sit down. I am Ruth Smith, the head teacher here. Horrible news about Val. Her husband rang me yesterday. I still can't believe it. Terrible.'

'How long had she worked here?'

'About three years, I think. Ever since she retired.'

'Retired?'

'Yes, she wanted to keep busy, she said.'

'And she retired from?'

'Nursing. She was a nurse.'

'Do you have a personnel file for her, please?'

'Well, I . . .'

'This is a murder inv—'

'Of course it is. Give me a second.'

Ruth Smith opened the top drawer of her desk and produced a set of keys. She then went to a filing cabinet in the corner of her office behind her desk and removed a thin file. She handed it to Dixon. 'Nothing very exciting, Inspector. Just a copy of her application form and contract. I don't recall any issues arising that would be recorded at all.'

'Was she here on Friday?'

'Yes. It was a normal day.' Ruth Smith's eyes welled up with tears. 'A perfectly normal day.'

'Who did she work with?'

'We had two dinner ladies. Val, of course, and Anne Brooks. They were both here on Friday.'

'Is Anne here now?'

'It's a bit early but she might be in the kitchen.'

'I'd like to speak to her, if I may?'

'Yes, certainly.'

'This may sound like a daft question to ask about a primary school dinner lady, but can you think of anyone who may have wished to do her harm? A parent, perhaps?'

'You obviously never met her, Inspector.'

'Sadly, no.'

'It's difficult to imagine meeting a nicer person. She never had a falling out with anyone, let alone one of the parents.'

'I understand. We have to ask.'

'Of course you do,' replied Ruth Smith. 'Is it true she was de . . . decap . . . ?'

'Yes, I'm afraid it is,' replied Dixon.

'Oh, my God.'

'Have the children been told?' asked Jane.

'No, not yet. I am liaising with the local education authority about how best to do that.'

'Can we speak to Anne now, please? I'd also like to keep this file, if that's all right,' said Dixon.

'Er, yes, that should be fine. Follow me.'

———

Anne Brooks was chopping lettuce in the kitchen. She was in her early sixties with tightly permed dark hair.

'Annie, these are two police officers. They'd like to have a word with you about Val . . .'

Anne Brooks immediately burst into tears. She began sobbing uncontrollably. Her legs went from under her and she fell forward onto the work surface. Ruth Smith put her arms around her while Dixon fetched a chair from the adjacent dining area.

'Another time,' said Dixon. 'We'll leave you to it.'

'You'll be back?' asked Ruth Smith.

'We will,' replied Dixon.

They could hear Anne Brooks still sobbing as they walked along the corridor to the exit.

———

'What did you make of Anne Brooks' reaction, Jane?' asked Dixon.

'You're not seriously suggesting . . .'

'What? Two dinner ladies have an argument and one cuts the other's head off? No, I meant did you think her reaction was genuine?'

'Yes, I did, actually,' replied Jane.

'So did I,' said Dixon. 'Has the FLO set up a meeting with the sisters yet?'

'I'll check,' said Jane, reaching into her handbag for her mobile phone.

Dixon drove along Coast Road and parked in Manor Way opposite Berrow Church. He could see the search still going on. He could also see three large white vans with satellite dishes on top, signwritten BBC, Sky News and ITN. He could hear a helicopter overhead. He looked and could see that it was private rather than police. Probably hired by one of the news agencies to get aerial shots of the search, Dixon thought.

He could hear Jane's telephone call coming to an end.

'Well?'

'One sister lives in Brisbane,' said Jane, looking at Dixon.

'Don't even think about it.'

'The other lives in Woolavington.'

'Doesn't quite have the same ring to it, does it?'

'No, but she's agreed to see us at 10.30 a.m.'

Lockswell Cottage, Woolavington, was a small double fronted stone cottage on the main road through the village. Dixon parked in Higher Road, a side road opposite the cottage, and watched the net curtains moving in the front window. He knocked on the door just before 10.30 a.m. A small dog started barking.

'Mrs Sheila Cummins?'

'Yes.'

'I'm Detective Inspector Dixon and this is Detective Constable Winter. You're expecting us, I believe?'

'Please, come in.'

'I hope you don't mind me saying so but you bear a striking resemblance to your sister, Mrs Cummins,' said Dixon.

'We're twins, Inspector. Were twins, I should say. Not quite identical, but almost.'

'I gather you know what happened to Mrs Manning?'

'Peter rang me last night, yes. Please sit down.'

The front door opened straight into the lounge. Dixon sat on an armchair. Jane sat next to Mrs Cummins on the sofa, opposite a large open fire.

'How would you describe your sister's relationship with her husband, Mrs Cummins?'

'I'm sure you know all about that already.'

'We know what Mr Manning has told us but I would like to know what you think.'

'It was good once. Then they got divorced. I know that he hit her, although she always denied it. It was difficult with them being stuck in the same house.'

'And recently?'

'They'd arrived at an understanding. She kept out of his way and he kept out of hers. They lived separate lives, as far as one can, living in the same house.'

'And your relationship with her, how would you describe that?'

'Not as close as we were once, I suppose. We grew apart as we got older. At least, that's how it felt.'

'Did you see much of her?'

'Not recently. I can't think why, really. And now it's too late . . .'

Tears began to stream down her cheeks.

'Jane, make Mrs Cummins a cup of tea,' said Dixon.

'No, I'm fine, really,' said Sheila Cummins. 'Did she suffer?'

'No.' Dixon lied again. 'Tell me about your other sister.'

'Emily. She's our elder sister. She married an Australian in the early eighties and went to live out there. We rarely see her these days, for obvious reasons. I haven't told her yet. She'll want to come for the funeral.'

'Did Valerie ever tell you she was in any sort of danger or in fear for her life, perhaps?'

'What an odd question.'

'It sounds it, I know. I'm just trying to rule things out at this stage. Can you think of anyone who may have wished her harm?'

'Certainly not!' said Sheila Cummins.

'What about her husband?' asked Jane.

'No. Surely you can't think that?'

'As I say, we are just trying to rule things out at this stage. Routine questions. By the book, as it were,' said Dixon.

'Well, you're barking up the wrong tree there.'

'And what about you? Are you married?'

'My husband died two years ago. Prostate cancer.'

'I'm sorry to hear that.'

'When you reach fifty, Inspector, have your PSA level checked at least once a year. My husband didn't and paid the price for it.'

'I'll try to remember that,' said Dixon.

'Make sure you do,' said Sheila Cummins. Tears began to stream down her cheeks again.

'We've taken up enough of your time, Mrs Cummins. If you think of anything that might be relevant, anything at all, please give me a ring. Here's my number,' said Dixon, placing his card on the coffee table.

'I will.'

Dixon and Jane got up to leave. A Yorkshire terrier came running into the lounge from the kitchen and jumped onto Sheila Cummins' lap. It began licking the tears from her cheeks.

'We'll show ourselves out.'

'C'mon, Jane, there's a park over there. Let's take Monty for a walk. We've got ten minutes.'

Dixon got Monty out of the back of the Land Rover and put his lead on. They crossed the road and walked the hundred yards or so along Lockswell to the small park.

'What do you make of it, then?' asked Dixon, letting Monty off the lead.

'I don't think the husband did it, which leaves us with a primary school dinner lady, who everyone says is lovely, being stabbed to death and then beheaded. I don't know, could it have been random?' asked Jane.

'No, it couldn't. It's Dixon's law. There's no such thing as a random killing.'

'Dixon's law?'

'I made that bit up. But there's always a reason . . .'

'Always?'

'Even a psychopath has a reason for selecting his victims.'

'I suppose so.'

'It may appear random, but there will be one somewhere, even if it's twisted.'

'True.'

'Trouble is, it becomes much harder to find if it only exists in the killer's head.'

'No shit.'

'It'll be there, though. We just have to find it.'

'Where?'

'Well, if it's not in Valerie's present, it must be in her past.'

'Could the killer have intended to kill Sheila Cummins?' asked Jane. They are almost identical twins after all?'

'Mistaken identity, you mean?'

'Yes.'

'You've been watching too much telly.'

Jane nodded in Monty's direction. 'You have some clearing up to do.'

Dixon reached into his coat pocket and produced a small black plastic bag. 'One of the joys of dog ownership. You get used to it.'

'We do a lot of that in this job, don't we?'

'We do. We certainly do.'

Dixon walked across to the dog bin. He turned to see Jane throwing a stick for Monty.

'Let's get back to the station,' said Dixon.

They walked back to the Land Rover. Dixon put Monty in the back, sat in the driver's seat and was about to switch on the engine when his phone rang.

'Dixon.'

'It's Sergeant Dean, Sir. We've found a bag in the undergrowth between the green and the church.'

'Is it . . . ?'

'There's blood, Sir. Lots of it. One of the dogs found it.'

'Any sign of a belt?'

'There's a leather belt in the bag.'

'We're on our way, Sergeant. Thank you.'

Dixon arrived at Berrow Church to find the Scientific Services van already there. He parked next to it and followed the track around to the right with Jane. They walked up to the twelfth green and could see a group of officers standing on the path that led from the green back to the gap in the wall at the top of the churchyard. The undergrowth on either side of the path was thick and consisted of several large bushes, of a type that Dixon could not identify, and thick brambles. They appeared to form a circle, with the interior being almost clear of all but long grass.

The officers stood back to allow Dixon a clear view into the undergrowth. An opening had been cut and he could see the senior scenes of crime officer, Watson, crouched over what looked like a black bag lying in the long grass.

'What've we got, then?'

'A black leather holdall. There's lots of congealed blood in it. We'll get a sample straight off to Dr Poland for analysis, but you don't have to be a rocket scientist to guess whose it is.'

'No,' replied Dixon. 'Anything else?'

'Yes, there's a brown leather belt in the bag. Not a pretty sight.'

Dixon turned to Jane and nodded.

'Any logos or anything like that?'

'I can see a Fat Face label on the belt and the bag has a Footjoy logo on it.'

'Our man's a golfer, then,' said Jane.

'Footjoy make ladies' golf shoes as well, Jane,' replied Dixon.

Jane shrugged her shoulders.

Sergeant Dean appeared behind Dixon.

'Mr Durkin has arrived, Sir, and would like a word.'

'What have you got left to do, Sergeant?'

'Very little, Sir. We're almost finished and are just winding down.'

'Has the undergrowth been checked that side?' asked Dixon, pointing to the other side of the path.

'Yes, Sir. We've had two dogs all over it.'

'So, I can tell Mr Durkin we'll be finished today and he can have his course back tomorrow?'

'Yes, Sir.'

Dixon walked back to the twelfth green. Paul Durkin was sitting in a golf buggy on the far side of the green. He got out and walked over to Dixon.

'Haven't you finished yet, Inspector?'

'Almost, Mr Durkin. We're just winding down, as it happens. There'll be some delay, though. We've found some items in the undergrowth back there that will need to be removed carefully. That may take some time.'

'Not into a third day, surely?'

'Mercifully not. The course can reopen tomorrow.'

'Thank heavens for that. This has caused a great deal of inconvenience, Inspector.'

'When I catch the killer, Mr Durkin, I'll be sure to pass that on.'

Dixon walked back over to where Jane was standing.

'C'mon, Jane, let's go and get something to eat.'

'Where?'

'The Berrow Inn will be full of journalists. How about the Red Cow?'

It was just after 2.30 p.m. when Dixon rang the bell on the locked front door of Lester Hodson Solicitors in Bridgwater. It was a two storey double fronted Georgian building that had been converted into offices. The large front door was painted black and there was a polished brass plaque on the wall to the left, listing the partners in the firm. The lock gave out a familiar buzzing sound, prompting Jane to push open the door. Once they were inside, a sign with an arrow pointing to the left led them to the reception desk.

'Detective Inspector Dixon and Detective Constable Jane Winter to see Anne Barton, please?' said Dixon. He produced his warrant card, as usual.

'Is she expecting you?'

'One of her clients was murdered yesterday so she should be, yes.'

'No, I mean do you have an appointment?'

'I think you'll find we don't need one.'

'Do sit down,' said the receptionist.

'We'll stand, if you don't mind. I don't expect Miss Barton to keep us waiting.'

The receptionist picked up the telephone and dialled a three digit extension number. She spoke so quietly that Dixon thought it unlikely that the person on the other end could have heard what was being said. Dixon certainly couldn't. He was assured that Miss Barton would be straight down to see them.

A few moments later, a door at the back of the reception area opened.

'Can I help you?'

Dixon turned to see a tall, smartly dressed woman wearing a grey two piece suit and white blouse. She had short blonde hair and was, Dixon thought, in her late forties.

'I am Anne Barton. You'll be here about Valerie Manning?'

'Yes. Is there anywhere we can . . . ?'

'Of course. Do come through.'

Dixon and Jane followed Anne Barton through to an interview room behind the reception area. Anne Barton and Jane sat either side of the desk. Dixon stood in the window looking out at the River Parrett, which ran behind the offices.

'You'll appreciate that I am bound by client confidentiality, Inspector.'

'I'm afraid all of that stuff goes out the window in a murder investigation, Miss Barton.'

'Well, I shall certainly help in any way that I can.'

'Thank you.'

'Is it true that she was . . . ?'

'It is, I'm afraid.'

'Good God.'

'We are just building a picture of Mrs Manning at this stage, and I have a fair idea of what you are going to say, I think. But can you tell me about her relationship with her husband, Peter?'

'He was a bit of a bastard, actually. At least to begin with. He wanted the divorce. Valerie didn't. He'd met someone else. He eventually got her to start the divorce proceedings based on his adultery.'

Jane was taking notes.

'It was a very difficult time. He hit her a few times and, in the end, I made an application for an injunction to force him out of the matrimonial home.'

'What was the outcome of that?'

'He persuaded her to drop it before the hearing and things have been largely quiet ever since. I think it caused the break up of his new relationship, actually.'

'The injunction?'

'Would you want to get involved with someone who was beating up his wife?' Anne Barton addressed the question to Jane.

'No,' she replied.

'How long ago was this?'

'Must be nearly three years ago. Been in limbo ever since. They agreed a fifty fifty split of everything but couldn't sell the house. It's quite common, that, at the moment. Leads to all sorts of problems.'

'Can we have a copy of the witness statement Mrs Manning gave in support of the injunction application?'

Jane looked across at Dixon, who was now standing by the fireplace at the side of the desk.

'I'll need to run that by my managing partner, but I don't see why not. Can I email it to you?'

'That'd be fine,' said Dixon, handing his calling card to Anne Barton.

'I'll try to do it this afternoon or perhaps tomorrow, if that's OK?'

'Thank you. You've been very helpful.'

Dixon called in at Bridgwater Police Station to check his post and emails. The police station was a purpose built red brick and glass building that could best be described as functional. His office was on the second floor adjacent to the CID Room.

Dixon was standing at the coffee machine when DCI Lewis appeared behind him.

'Any news, Nick?'

'We've found the bag with the belt in it, Sir. It's a black holdall with a Footjoy logo on it. The belt is leather and comes from Fat Face. There's a lot of blood congealed in the bottom of the bag and a sample is on its way to Roger Poland.'

'Anything else?'

'Nothing substantive. We've spoken to the head teacher at Berrow School and also Valerie Manning's sister in Woolavington. The other sister lives in Australia. I was hoping to speak to the work colleague in the kitchens at the school but couldn't get a word out of her, unfortunately.'

'And?'

'Getting a picture of a lovely lady who wouldn't say boo to a goose. No one can imagine why anyone would wish to do her harm at all, it seems. Her solicitor gave an interesting insight into the divorce proceedings and the domestic violence but even that was three years ago. I've asked her to let me have a copy of the witness statement that Mrs Manning gave in support of the application for an injunction.'

'An injunction?'

'Yes. Apparently the violence got so bad at one point that Mrs Manning tried to get her husband out of the house. He persuaded her to drop the proceedings, though, and things have been calm ever since. The solicitor thinks that Peter Manning was seeing someone else, hence the divorce, and the injunction application put an end to that relationship.'

'Well, keep me posted.'

'Will do, Sir. It'll be interesting to see what Dave and Mark come up with. There's a briefing at 6 p.m., if you can make it.'

'I won't be able to get there, unfortunately, but let me know how you get on.'

'Will do.'

'The chief superintendent seems to think you are an officer who makes things happen, Nick.'

'I'll do my best, Sir.'

Dixon sat at his desk with his coffee and logged into his computer. It was a small office that he shared with DCI Janice Courtenay. She had left a note on his desk telling him that she would be on holiday for the next two weeks. Dixon screwed it up and threw it in the rubbish bin.

He opened his emails to find two hundred and seventy-nine new messages. For the most part, each email represented a telephone call received from members of public following the Sunday evening press conference. Dixon looked at his watch. It was just after 4 p.m., giving him an hour and a half before he would need to leave to get back to Burnham for the 6 p.m. briefing.

He reached over and switched on his printer. He then began opening the emails in chronological order, beginning on the Sunday evening. It quickly became apparent that very few contained any useful information. A central record would be kept of each message received, so Dixon deleted from his computer those that were not relevant. The usual cranks, nutters and those whose information was either irrelevant or clearly wrong. He also deleted all internal police newsletters and memoranda. Although not technically junk mail, he regarded them as such and took great delight in hitting the delete button.

By 4.30 p.m. he had narrowed it down to fifty-nine emails that would require closer scrutiny. His attention was drawn to a telephone message received at 10.27 p.m. on the Sunday—just after the evening news, he thought. The witness, Daniel Fisher, said that he was driving from Burnham-on-Sea to Brean in the early hours of Sunday morning when he had seen a car turning out of the track that leads to Berrow Church. Fisher had been to a nightclub in Burnham and was on his way home. Dixon made a note to follow up this sighting. Otherwise, the messages were of very little interest apart from one timed at 3.23 p.m. that day. The male caller had not left his name and number. The message read simply 'Vodden 1979'. Dixon hit the delete button.

He turned off his computer and printer, having printed off only one email. It was disappointing but there was, at least, a possible sighting of the killer.

Dixon shouted across to Jane, who was sitting at her computer in the CID room.

'Did you see anything interesting in those emails, Jane?'

'Not really, apart from the obvious one, of course.'

'Daniel Fisher?'

'Yes.'

'Give him a ring and see if he can see us this evening.'

'Will do.'

A few minutes later, Jane appeared in the doorway of Dixon's office.

'He works shifts and is on nights at the moment. He can see us in the morning, though. I've made an appointment to see him at home at 8.30.'

'Good. C'mon, we need to get to Burnham.'

The incident room on the second floor of Burnham-on-Sea Police Station was a hive of activity when Dixon and Jane arrived for the briefing just before 6 p.m. Dave Harding and Mark Pearce were staring intently at a television screen, and various other officers, who had been drafted in to assist the investigation, were either answering telephones or reviewing CCTV footage on their computers. Dixon sat on the edge of an empty desk next to the whiteboard and called the briefing to order.

'Good evening, everyone. As you know, we've found the holdall and belt, so it seems Dr Poland was right about the mechanics. I'm just waiting for his formal report. We also have a sighting of a car turning out of the Berrow Church car park in the early hours of Sunday morning. Jane and I will be interviewing the witness in the morning. Dave, what have you come up with?'

'We spoke to the friends Valerie went to the theatre with and got detailed statements from them both. They're being typed up now.' Dave looked at his notebook, 'Mrs Emily Townsend of 17 Margaret Crescent, that's off South Esplanade in Burnham. An old work colleague of Valerie's, apparently. Anyway, she drove. She picked Valerie up in the Morrisons car park at the top of Pier Street and then picked up Mrs Claire Stewart at her home in Stoddens Road. That was on their way out to the motorway, of course.'

'So, Valerie's car was left unattended all evening in the car park?'

'Yes, Sir.'

'There should be CCTV coverage, then?'

'There is. I'll come on to that in a second,' said Harding. 'They went to see *The Lion King* at the Hippodrome and left Bristol just after 11 p.m. They dropped Mrs Stewart at home and then Mrs Townsend dropped Valerie off in Pier Street at about 11.45 p.m.'

'She didn't drop her at her car?' asked Dixon.

'No, sadly not. She pulled up in the bus stop opposite the Pier Tavern and left Valerie to walk to her car.'

'Did she wait and see if Valerie got to her car?'

'No, she didn't, I'm afraid. She drove off. She last saw Valerie walking across the pavement by the bus stop.'

'Talk about seeing to it that your friend gets home safely,' said Dixon.

'She knows that now, Sir.'

'Bit bloody late, isn't it, Dave?'

'Yes, Sir.'

'What happens next?' asked Dixon.

'This is where we pick it up on CCTV. Mark, wind the film back to when Mrs Townsend's car appears. Can everyone see this screen?'

Jane switched the lights off and then stood next to Dixon. Mark Pearce and Dave Harding were seated at the desk the screen was sitting on. The other officers in the room gathered around. Mark Pearce started the film.

The Morrisons car park was on the corner of Pier Street and the Esplanade. It was deserted apart from four cars, all parked in bays adjacent to Pier Street. The cars were clearly visible, there being no boundary fencing or bushes to screen the car park from either the road or the CCTV camera.

Dixon watched a red Mazda 6 estate car appear in the bus stop and Valerie Manning get out of the front passenger seat. She leaned back into the car and exchanged words with the driver, then she closed the door and turned to walk across the pavement.

'Stop the tape,' said Dixon. 'What does she say to Mrs Townsend?'

'Just goodbye and thank you, that's all. Nothing of any significance.'

Dixon looked at the bus stop. It was of stone construction, rather than glass, with a pitched roof and wood cladding to the front gable end. It was open at the front, although sideways on to the prevailing wind. There was a bench along the back wall. It was empty.

'OK, start the film.'

'This is where it gets interesting, Sir,' said Pearce.

'That's Valerie's car there,' said Harding, pointing to a red Fiat Uno parked three spaces up from the bus stop. 'Now, watch the back of the bus stop.'

Dixon could feel his pulse quicken. He had a clear understanding of what was about to happen. He could feel beads of sweat on his forehead and in the small of his back. He watched Valerie Manning walking across to her car. She was looking down, fumbling for her car keys in her handbag.

Suddenly, a figure appeared from behind the bus stop. He or she was wearing dark trousers and a dark coat with the hood up, obscuring the face. A blade glinted in the streetlights.

'Stop the tape,' said Dixon.

'Are there any other cameras that might give a view of the back of the bus stop?'

'No, Sir. We're getting this from the Reeds Arms, the Wetherspoon pub opposite. There's another camera on the Tourist Information Centre by the jetty, but this is the better angle.'

'OK, Mark.'

Pearce started the film. The figure had almost reached Valerie Manning before she turned. Soft shoes, thought Dixon. The figure slashed at Valerie with the knife. She dropped her handbag and clasped the back of her left hand with her right. She stumbled back against the driver's door of her car. The figure was waving the knife in front of her. He or she then pointed the knife at the handbag on the ground. Valerie stepped forward, bent down and picked it up. Then she was fumbling for her keys again. Greater urgency this time.

'Stop the tape.'

Pearce obliged.

'Any views on whether that's a man or a woman?' asked Dixon.

'Looks female to me, Sir.'

Dixon turned to the WPC who had spoken. 'And you are?'

'WPC Willmott, Sir. We met on Berrow Beach.'

'Of course we did. Why do you think it's female then?'

'Size, stature, the way it's holding the knife . . .'

'Explain.'

'A man would stand tall. Look at her. She's almost crouching behind the knife, holding it up at Mrs Manning.'

Dixon nodded.

'Look at the way she's holding it too. The palm of her hand is facing up.'

'It's pissing down with rain,' said Harding. 'Anyone would be hunched over, surely?'

'And nervous,' said Pearce.

'What you're saying, then, is that it could be male or female?'

'Well, there's nothing obvious that leaps out at you, is there, Sir?' said Jane.

'Do we ever get a clear view of the face, Dave?'

'No, Sir, sadly not.'

'Well, for present purposes we'll refer to the killer as 'he'. Start the tape, Mark.'

They watched while Valerie found her keys and opened the car. A prod of the knife and she climbed into the driver's seat. The figure opened the back door, threw a holdall into the back and then got into the passenger seat behind her. They could see the figure raise his arms and reach forward over the driver's seat. Valerie

Manning lurched back into her seat. Her head thrashing to the left and right.

'That's the belt going round her neck,' said Pearce.

The car then reversed slowly out of the parking space, turned and drove out of shot, heading towards the exit. Dixon's last view was of Valerie Manning driving with her assailant hunched in the back seat behind her.

'We don't see the car again on this camera, Sir,' said Harding.

'That means they must have gone along the sea front?'

'Yes. There's footage of the car passing the jetty camera and going straight along the Esplanade rather than turning right into Pier Street.'

'But that's the last camera?'

'It is, Sir. There are no more between here and Berrow Beach.'

'Switch it off, will you, Mark? I've seen enough for the time being.'

Mark Pearce switched off the television and the officers returned to their seats. Dixon used the opportunity to pour himself a drink from the water tower.

'What time does Morrisons close on a Saturday?'

'9 p.m., Sir,' said WPC Willmott.

'So, the killer leaves his car at Berrow Church, in the overflow car park, well hidden from the road. He then, somehow, gets to Burnham, where he waits for Valerie to get back from the theatre. That means there is either an accomplice who gave the killer a lift or he took a bus or taxi. Dave, you know what to do?'

'Yes, Sir.'

'It's possible that he could have walked all the way along the beach, I suppose. What is it, four miles?'

'About that,' replied Willmott.

'Well, let's try the buses and taxis anyway, Dave.'

Harding nodded.

'Let's assume that he arrived in Burnham early and waited in or around Morrisons until Valerie got back. I want the Reeds Arms and the jetty cameras checked from 4 p.m. onwards. You know what you are looking for. We'll also need two officers outside Morrisons until we find someone who saw something on Saturday evening. Speak to the regulars in the Reeds and the Pier Tavern too.'

'Yes, Sir,' said Harding.

'OK. Then, later, the killer cuts across the golf course back to Berrow Church. Leaves Valerie's head in the bunker on the way, throws the bag with the belt in it into the bushes and then drives home in his own car.'

'Covered in blood,' said Jane. 'Which explains the fainter trail leading from the bunker down through the churchyard to the car park.'

'Good point,' replied Dixon. 'Right, well, that's enough to be going on with, I think. Has everyone got a clear understanding of what they are doing tomorrow?'

'Yes, Sir.'

'Good. See you in the morning.'

Dixon saw Jane in the car park outside the police station.

'Are you . . . er . . .'

'I'm going to go back to my flat, if it's all the same to you. I need some clothes and stuff.'

'Yes, fine. See you tomorrow.'

Dixon arrived home just before 8 p.m. He had intended to take Monty for a walk on Burnham Beach, but fireworks were going off all around and he didn't want to risk him running off. Even a Staffie will be frightened on bonfire night. Instead, he opted for a quick walk on the lead around the roads in Brent Knoll, followed by beans on toast. He fed Monty, opened a can of beer and sat in the dark in his cottage, watching the flashes of rockets and Roman candles light up the room.

He was in for a restless night. He thought about Valerie Manning and the figure in the car park slashing at her with the knife. The image played over and over again in his mind like a short piece of film on a loop.

He switched on his television and reached for a DVD. His collection was small and universally regarded as awful by those who knew him. Places to go, rather than just films, he always said. He opted for his favourite, *Goodbye, Mr Chips*, finished his beer and was asleep before the opening credits had finished rolling.

Chapter Four

Dixon woke to the sound of knocking on his front door. He looked at his watch: 10.55 p.m. Monty woke up and started barking. *Goodbye, Mr Chips* had finished long ago, leaving the DVD menu on the screen and the Brookfield School song playing over and over.

Dixon opened the door to find Jane standing on his doorstep. She was carrying a bag.

'I changed my mind.'

'Come in,' said Dixon, moving to one side to allow Jane into his cottage.

'You said if it wasn't in her present, it must be in her past.'

'I did.'

'Get your computer out. I'll put the kettle on.'

Jane dropped her bag at the bottom of the stairs and looked at the television. 'What on earth is that?'

'*Goodbye, Mr Chips*. What's this all about?'

'I'll tell you in a minute.'

Dixon switched off the television and powered up his laptop. Jane appeared from the kitchen with a mug of tea in each hand.

'Go to Google.'

Dixon did as he was told. Jane handed him a mug and then sat on the arm of the sofa next to him.

'Right, now, search against Vodden 1979 and look at the very first result.'

Dixon looked quizzically at her. Jane nodded. He typed 'Vodden 1979' into the search field and hit the 'Enter' button. The search took 0.35 seconds and returned 1,620,000 results. It took a moment for the significance of what he was looking at to sink in. Dixon looked at Jane and then back to his computer screen. He was stunned. He read aloud.

'List of unsolved murders in the United Kingdom: Wikipedia, the free encyclopedia. 1979, Ralph Vodden; Royal West Norfolk Golf Club; on 4th November 1979 the body of Dr Ralph Vodden was found. He had been brutally . . .'

He looked at Jane and raised his eyebrows.

'Open it,' she said, 'and scroll down to 1979.'

Dixon clicked on the Wikipedia entry and waited for the page to load. Then he scrolled down. It was a long list, starting in 1752 with the murder of Colin Roy Campbell of Glenure. There were five entries for 1979. Again, he read aloud.

'1979, Ralph Vodden; Location body found, Royal West Norfolk Golf Club; Notes: On 4 November 1979 the body of Dr Ralph Vodden was found. He had been brutally murdered and then decapitated. He was last seen alive leaving his surgery on the evening of 3 November 1979. His body was found in a burnt out car on the beach at Holkham, Norfolk, and his head was found in a bunker on the Royal West Norfolk Golf Club. So far, nobody has been convicted of his murder.'

'It can't be a coincidence, can it?' asked Jane.

'No, it bloody well can't. What made you . . . ?'

'I just thought I'd Google it and see what came up.'

'Apart from the obvious, what else connects the two cases, then, clever clogs?'

'I don't know, you tell me.'

'Valerie Manning was a nurse and Ralph Vodden was a doctor. That leaps out at me. Apart from that, I can't think of anything.'

'Me neither.'

'I can tell you what we'll be doing tomorrow afternoon, though.'

'What?'

'Driving to Norfolk.'

***

Dixon knocked on the door of Daniel Fisher's bungalow in Warren Road, Brean, just after 8.30 a.m. It was situated on the coast road, fronting the road itself and backing onto the beach. It was midway between the village and Brean Down.

The bungalow was for sale and Dixon did not expect it to remain on the market for long. They would need to keep track of Daniel Fisher. He would no doubt be a key witness.

The bungalow itself was of red brick construction with a conservatory at the front that appeared to be perched on top of a double garage. Dixon thought it odd that the conservatory was at the front of the bungalow, facing inland, rather than at the back, looking out to sea.

The door was answered by a man in his early thirties. He was taller than Dixon, and slim, with short dark hair.

'We are looking for Daniel Fisher.'

'That's me. Come in.'

Dixon and Jane followed Daniel Fisher through to the kitchen at the back of the bungalow.

'I've just come in from work and am having a bite to eat.'

'That's fine, Mr Fisher. I'm Detective Inspector Nick Dixon and this is Detective Constable Jane Winter.'

'I'm not sure how much help I can be, to be honest. I didn't get a clear look at him, I'm afraid.'

'You said "him"?' asked Dixon.

'Just a figure of speech, I suppose. I couldn't really tell whether it was male or female.'

'OK. Well, let's start at the beginning. You'd been into Burnham for the evening?'

'Yes.'

Jane was handwriting a statement.

'I met some friends for a meal at the Zalshah. We had a few drinks in the Railway, the Pier and Reeds. Then we went to the club.'

'Is that Blue Sky's?'

'Yes.'

'What time did you leave?'

'About 1.30, I think. It had been a fairly boring evening, to be honest. I couldn't drink because I was driving.'

'What happened then?'

'I dropped two friends home on the way. They share a flat in Grove Road. Then I drove home.'

'What was the weather like?'

'It was pouring with rain and pitch dark, obviously.'

'Did you have your windscreen wipers on?'

'Yes. Not fast, though. Just normal speed.'

'Tell me what you saw then,' said Dixon.

'I'd just come round the bend at Berrow Church and saw a car turning out of the car park there. It was turning right towards Burnham. It just struck me as odd, that's all, with it being so late.'

'Did you see the driver?'

'Briefly.'

'What was he wearing?'

'Dark clothing, that's all I can say, really. A coat or jacket with a hood. It was up.'

'Did you see the face?'

'No, he had the hood up and was hunched over the steering wheel. He may also have looked away but I can't be sure.'

'What about the car?'

'Small and dark. Either dark blue or black, dark grey, perhaps. Newish. Possibly a Toyota Yaris or Nissan Micra. Something like that. It struck me as odd because he could only have been up to the church.'

'Did you see this person drive off?'

'I looked in my rear view mirror but didn't see anything, I'm afraid. I'd either missed him or he waited until I'd gone.'

'Is there anything else we've not covered?'

'Not that I can think of.'

'Well, if you think of anything else, please let us know straight away. We'll leave you to get some sleep. Where do you work?'

'Storey Juices over at Bridgwater. We make fruit juices and stuff.'

'I see your house is up for sale. Are you going far?'

'That's my parents. They're only planning to move into Burnham.'

'Let us know if you do change address, though,' said Dixon.

'I will.'

Jane had handwritten a short statement for Daniel Fisher, which he read and then signed at the bottom of each page. Once back in the Land Rover, Jane spoke first.

'Seems to confirm it?'

'Possibly. If it was the husband, though, why would he drive when he lives so close?'

'True,' said Jane.

'C'mon, let's call in at Burnham. Then we need to get to Norfolk.'

Dixon drove south along Coast Road heading towards Burnham-on-Sea. He turned right onto the beach road. This time there was no police constable in attendance or blue tape that needed to be removed. He drove past the Sundowner Cafe and out onto the beach. He turned south towards where Valerie Manning's Fiat Uno had been found.

'Where are we going?' asked Jane.

Dixon remained silent.

He parked the Land Rover facing out to sea, switched off the engine and then walked around the back to let Monty out for a run. Jane got out of the passenger side and walked round to the back just in time to see Monty take off in pursuit of his tennis ball.

'What's up?'

'I just wanted a minute to think,' said Dixon.

The tide was coming in and the waves were crashing through the hull of the SS *Nornen*.

'It looks like an old Viking longship, doesn't it?' said Jane.

'I always used to think it was, but it dates from the end of the nineteenth century. It ran aground in a storm.'

Dixon stood where Valerie Manning's car had been found.

'It was about here, wasn't it?'

The image of Valerie Manning and the killer in the car park flashed across Dixon's mind. He thought about what had happened on that spot only a few days before. He looked down and kicked the sand. Just then Monty appeared at his feet with his tennis ball in his mouth.

'That's a first,' said Jane. 'He's never brought the ball back before.'

'No, he hasn't,' said Dixon. He wrestled with Monty to loosen his grip on the ball. Eventually, Monty let go and Dixon threw it along the sand.

'Let's assume Doctor Vodden and Valerie Manning were killed by the same person. Why the long gap between the killings?' asked Dixon.

'There could be any number of reasons,' said Jane.

'There could. It might not even be the same person.'

'Same motive, then?'

'Must be. Decapitation is making one hell of a statement, isn't it?'

By mid-morning Dixon was driving north on the M5 in his Land Rover. Jane was sitting in the passenger seat and Monty was asleep in the back. DCI Lewis had agreed the trip and a meeting had been scheduled for 9 a.m. the following day with Detective Inspector Alan Dentus at Norfolk Police Headquarters, Wymondham, a few miles to the south-west of Norwich.

The file on the murder of Dr Ralph Vodden remained open but the case was not actively under investigation. The files were being retrieved from store that afternoon. At Dixon's insistence, a meeting had also been set up with the now retired Senior Investigating Officer, DCI John French, at his bungalow in Cromer.

Jane was searching the Internet on her phone, looking for accommodation for the night.

'There's a Premier Inn at Norwich.'

'They don't take dogs,' replied Dixon.

'Nobody's going to steal Monty, are they?'

'It's more likely, if anything. Dog fighting.'

'Oh, OK,' said Jane, turning back to her phone.

They drove on in silence, Jane trying to find them a room for the night, Dixon deep in thought.

'How about the Old Vicarage at Thetford? It's a B&B but they take dogs.'

'Sounds good to me,' replied Dixon. 'Don't forget to book two rooms.'

'Two?'

'The expenses claim will look a bit odd if we don't.'

Jane smiled. She rang the Old Vicarage and booked the rooms. Ten pounds extra for Monty.

'That's a bit steep, isn't it?' said Jane. 'Particularly as he won't use the bed or have breakfast.'

'He will. We just won't tell them that,' said Dixon.

They had reached Bristol before Dixon spoke again.

'Why do people kill each other, Jane?'

'Money, jealousy and revenge. It's usually one or more of those reasons, when it boils down to it.'

Dixon nodded and carried on driving. They turned east onto the M42 south of Birmingham and finally arrived in Norfolk just after 4 p.m. It was already starting to get dark, the clocks having gone back two weeks before. They checked in at the Old Vicarage and then walked to the local pub for supper. It came highly recommended and allowed dogs, which was an added bonus.

'You never told me how you won the Police Medal,' said Jane.

'I didn't.'

'Well?'

'No, I didn't win the Queen's Police Medal.'

'You said . . .'

'I won the George Medal.'

'How?'

'Long story.'

'We've got all night.'

'Actually, it's not a long story at all. I'd nipped into M&S for a sandwich. Heard a shotgun blast, came out, and there's a man on other side of the road with a shotgun. He had a motorcycle helmet on and he'd just come out of the bookmakers. Someone followed him out and he shot them in the legs, then made for a motorbike that was parked on the corner.'

'So what did you do?'

'I ran across the road and rugby tackled him. We crashed through the window of Starbucks and that was that, really.'

'You tackled an armed man?'

'I didn't think it was a big deal at the time. It was a double barrelled shotgun and he'd fired one barrel in the bookies and the other outside, so I thought he was out of ammo.'

'And?'

'I found out later that he'd fired both barrels in the bookies and then reloaded before he came out. I nearly shit myself.'

Jane was laughing so much she started choking on her wine.

'Turned out it was a hit. Anyway, that's it, really.' Dixon reached over and patted Jane on the back. She stopped coughing and took a sip of wine.

'The accidental hero. Isn't that a film?' she said.

'Piss off.'

Norfolk Police Headquarters, Wymondham, was a large red brick complex nine miles south-west of Norwich. There were several buildings on the site, including the operations and communications centre, apparent from the aerials and radio masts on the roof, and the main office building. They were greeted in reception by DI Alan Dentus and, after the usual formalities, were shown to a meeting room on the first floor with large windows overlooking the car park.

There were three document archive boxes on the table and a photocopier in the corner. DI Dentus spoke only to offer tea or coffee and to confirm that he had no personal knowledge of the Vodden case whatsoever. It had been 'done and dusted' long before his time, apparently. He also gave Dixon a telephone extension number to ring when they had finished and he would come down and show them out. He switched on the photocopier and then left them to it.

'You start that end, Jane. I'll start this end and meet you in the middle. Photocopy anything that looks interesting.'

Dixon opened the archive box in front of him. It contained a number of blue folders, each no more than an inch think. He removed the one nearest to him and looked at the label: 'Witness Statements'. The first came from a member of the greens staff at the Royal West Norfolk Golf Club. He had found Dr Vodden's severed head in a greenside bunker on the twelfth hole. Dixon did not think it odd that a greenkeeper had found it. They would usually be the first out on the course in the morning. It was clearly significant that it had been found on the twelfth hole, and he placed the statement to one side to be photocopied. Next he found a statement from a dog walker who had found the burnt out car on Holkham Beach. He added it to the pile to be photocopied.

'What've you got, Jane?'

'Telephone call log. Nothing exciting.'

Dixon turned back to the witness statements. He found a statement from Dr Vodden's widow. She had last seen her husband that morning and knew of no one who might have wanted to kill him. There were several from other doctors at the surgery where Dr Vodden had been working. He had been there six months and was working as a locum. Dixon decided to photocopy all of the statements in the folder, and set them to one side. He then added Dr Vodden's NHS file to the pile to be copied.

The next folder contained interview transcripts and was the thickest of the folders by some considerable margin. It seemed that any and every local man with a history of violence had been pulled in for interview. The investigation clearly lacked any significant leads, even early on, and any likely culprit was arrested and brought in. Dixon closed the folder and put it back in the box.

He knew he would need to copy the contents of the third folder but opened it and read it anyway. It was the Home Office pathologist's report. He turned to the conclusions and read aloud.

'Cause of death 1(a) Myocardial infarction caused by stab wound to the heart; and 1(b) Desanguination caused by laceration to the neck severing the carotid artery.'

'What's desanguination?' asked Jane.

'Massive blood loss. Listen to this,' said Dixon. 'The head was then severed from the body post mortem.'

'Well, that's no coincid—'

'Significant contusion to the front of the neck consistent with restraint, possibly to the car seat headrest. Did car seats have headrests in those days?'

'We'll soon find out. What was he driving?' asked Jane.

Dixon flicked through the witness statements. 'A Rover 3500.'

Jane reached for her phone and opened the web browser. A quick search of Google images confirmed that the Rover 3500 did indeed have headrests.

'This cannot be a coincidence,' said Jane.

'Did you ever think it was?'

By 11.30 a.m. they had finished going through the boxes and had photocopied all of the documents and witness statements they thought remotely relevant. Dixon also kept two bound sets of photographs, hiding them in amongst his papers. He rang Alan Dentus, who arrived to show them out.

'Do you happen to know if the widow is still alive?'

'No, she died. I can tell you that. About ten years ago, maybe.'

'And the children?'

'Didn't know he had any.'

Dixon and Jane signed out of Norfolk Police Headquarters and walked over to the Land Rover. Half an hour later they were driving north on the B1149.

'You've gone the wrong way. We need the A140 for Cromer,' said Jane.

'We're not going to Cromer, Jane.'

'Where are we going?'

'Holkham Beach.'

Dixon turned off the A149 opposite Holkham Hall, home to the Earl of Leicester, and drove along Lady Anne's Drive. It was a tree lined avenue leading straight to the beach that was once the private beach access for the Hall. He parked on the grass verge at the end and let Monty out of the back.

'C'mon, Jane. We've got time. We're not due at Cromer till 2.30.'

They walked out through the Holkham National Nature Reserve and onto the beach. The tide was out, revealing a vast expanse of sand, far bigger even than Berrow. An icy north wind was blowing onshore, straight off the North Sea, and it was bitterly cold.

'Where was his car found?' asked Jane. 'I'm assuming that's why we're here.'

'Over there,' said Dixon, pointing back behind them. 'Monty needs a run. We've got six hours in the car ahead of us.'

They turned and walked back to the gate at the end of Lady Anne's Drive. Dixon then turned east and walked for one hundred yards along the edge of the nature reserve. He stopped and turned to Jane.

'This is where his car was found.'

Thick marsh grass extended out towards the beach. Inland, between the reserve and the road, were pine trees. Plenty of cover to screen a car fire.

'Does the tide reach this high?' asked Jane.

'Don't know,' replied Dixon. 'Does it matter?'

'No, I don't suppose it does.'

'Let's get to Cromer for some fish and chips.'

———

Number 87 Burnt Hills, Cromer, was a small grey stone bungalow with white painted wood cladding at the front. There was a drive leading to a single garage with a white painted door. Dixon parked in the drive.

The garden was immaculate, which told Dixon that the occupant was retired, but then he knew that anyway. The door was answered by a woman in her late seventies with grey hair.

'Come in. My husband's expecting you. He's in the conservatory.'

Dixon and Jane followed her through to the rear of the bungalow.

'Would you like a cup of tea?'

'That would be lovely, thank you,' said Dixon.

'Yes, please,' said Jane.

They walked into the conservatory and were greeted by a tall man with thinning grey hair. He wore red corduroys, a shirt open at the neck and a cardigan. He looked them up and down.

'You two got here pretty damn quick.'

'Vodden 1979?' asked Dixon.

'Yes, that was me. How did you . . . ?'

'Google,' said Jane.

'I'm John French, retired detective chief inspector. Twenty years now.' He shook hands with Dixon and Jane, who introduced themselves.

'What've you got, then?' he asked.

'A sixty-eight year old woman. Murdered. Decapitated. Body found in a burnt out car on the beach and her head in a greenside bunker on the twelfth hole at Burnham and Berrow Golf Club,' said Dixon.

'Have you been to Wymondham?'

'This morning.'

'Then you've seen Dr Vodden's post mortem report.'

'Almost identical.'

'Fucking hell.'

'I heard that.' Mrs French appeared in the doorway with a tray of tea, which she placed on the glass coffee table in the conservatory. There were chocolate biscuits on a plate too.

Dixon and Jane were sitting on a two seat bamboo sofa. John French sat down in an armchair opposite them.

'I'll pour the tea, Iris, don't worry,' said French.

'Thank you very much, Mrs French,' said Dixon.

'What did Valerie Manning do for a living?' asked French.

'She was a primary school dinner lady.'

Jane looked at Dixon. He nodded. She said nothing.

'Tell me about the Vodden murder,' said Dixon.

'It was my first case as a DCI and it broke my heart. It went cold on me almost straight away. No sightings, no witnesses, nothing. We didn't have CCTV and DNA in those days, of course.'

'What about Dr Vodden?'

'We went back through his personal life, work life, everything. And came up with nothing. He had no money worries, was happily married and no issues at work. We came to the conclusion it was some random psycho.'

'It happens,' said Dixon.

'I always thought he'd kill again. Never thought he'd wait this long, though.'

'He?'

'It's got to be a man. A woman could never do that.'

'The CCTV footage we have is inconclusive,' said Jane.

'I kept in touch with the widow for years but never had any positive news for her. She died in 2004. Cancer.'

'Children?' asked Dixon.

'There were two, aged eight and eleven at the time. The daughter married an American and went to live in Washington. The son emigrated to New Zealand. That was the last straw for their mother, I think.'

'Where was Dr Vodden living?'

'Sheringham. A nice house overlooking the sea.'

'Where was he working at the time?'

'He was a locum at a surgery here in Cromer, as it happens. He'd been there for six months.'

'And before that?'

'He was at a surgery in Norwich, from memory, and maybe Thetford as well before that. He was doing locum work, which is not unusual for doctors.'

'And you didn't find anything unusual in his work history?'

'Nothing at all. No money problems, partnership disputes, nothing. We went right back through all of the patients he had dealt with, too, and found nothing of interest.'

'How far did you go back?'

'Right back to when he first moved to Norfolk. About three years, as far as I can remember.'

'What were you looking for in his patient histories then?'

'Anything unusual, really. Relationship with a patient, misdiagnosis, that sort of thing. There really was absolutely nothing at all. By all accounts, he was an excellent doctor.'

'Are any of the other doctors still alive?'

'Yes. At least one is still practising here in Cromer.'

'I may need to speak to them in due course.'

'That shouldn't be a problem,' said French. 'What are you thinking?'

'The murders are almost identical. That tells me that either the killer or the motive, or both, for that matter, are the same. It's possible that the killer may be different, given that the murders are over thirty years apart, but the motive for each killing must surely be the same.'

'Which means that there must be a connection between Valerie Manning and Dr Vodden?'

'There is,' said Dixon. 'What I didn't tell you is that although Valerie Manning was a school dinner lady, she was also a retired nurse. At some point her path must have crossed with Dr Vodden's. Find that point and we find the motive.'

'It's the obvious connection,' said French.

'It is,' replied Dixon. 'You mentioned that you went back through his work history to when he moved to Norfolk?'

'Yes.'

'Where was he before that?'

'Burnham-on-Sea.'

Chapter Five

Dixon arrived home just before midnight and, despite over six hours in the car, managed to get very little sleep. He spent most of the night pacing up and down in the dark or drinking tea. By 6.30 a.m. he was on Berrow Beach with Monty. It was a clear and crisp morning with the faintest of breezes. The tide was coming in and the waves were rolling up the beach rather than crashing, making barely a sound. He watched the sun rise to the east just before 7 a.m. to reveal a clear blue sky.

Dixon had parked by the Sundowner Cafe and walked out to where Valerie Manning's car had been found. He was convinced of the connection between her murder and that of Ralph Vodden. He was also conscious of the need to keep the investigation moving forward. A wrong turn now and it might go cold on him, as it had done to DCI French in 1979.

A nurse and a doctor. Dixon had decided their paths must have crossed before 1976 when Dr Vodden had moved from Burnham to Norfolk. It could, perhaps, have been later but that was unlikely. The search would begin in 1976 and work back in time from there. If that produced nothing then it could always be widened. Both were happily married at the time, by all accounts, so it was unlikely that their connection would have been a personal one. Still possible, of course, but unlikely. That left work, and what connects a doctor and a nurse? That was not such an easy question to answer. He thought about the possibilities. Drugs, perhaps, theft of hospital property, money; he ruled them out one by one. The most likely one was the most obvious one. A patient.

He looked at his watch. 7.20 a.m. Then he looked at his feet. He was standing in two inches of water. He climbed up onto the sand dunes and walked back to his car. Monty opted to paddle back along the beach to the Land Rover. They were back at Dixon's cottage in Brent Knoll by 8 a.m. Jane was still asleep.

Dixon fed Monty and was eating a bowl of cornflakes when Jane appeared at the top of the stairs. She was wearing his dressing gown.

'How long have you been up?'

'Since about two o'clockish,' replied Dixon. 'Couldn't sleep. Coffee?'

'Yes, please.'

Dixon went into the kitchen and put the kettle on. Jane sat on the sofa.

'How long have we got?'

'Plenty of time. I've scheduled a briefing for 9 a.m.'

'What's the plan?' asked Jane.

'We start in 1976 and work back.'

'What are we looking for?'

'Patients. At some point before Vodden left for Norfolk in 1976, they were both involved in treating the same patient or patients.'

'That's quite an assumption.'

'I prefer to call it a leap of faith. But something happened; something went wrong. And I'm guessing it's the reason Vodden left for Norfolk. I'd love to be able to speak to his widow but can't.'

'She may not have known the real reason anyway.'

'I want Valerie's complete NHS personnel file. We can start by comparing it to Vodden's. And access to his patient records from his surgery in Burnham.'

'We don't even know which one he was at yet.'

'That should be in the personnel file we brought back from Norfolk. And we'll need to speak to any of the other doctors who are still alive. See if they remember anything.'

'What about patient confidentiality?'

'Fuck that.'

⌣

The briefing had already begun by the time Jane arrived at Burnham Police Station. She had driven over in her own car, having left Dixon's cottage ten minutes after him to avoid arriving together.

'Come in, Jane,' said Dixon. 'You're late.'

She glared at him from the back of the CID room.

'I was just bringing everyone up to date on the Norfolk developments.'

'Yes, Sir.'

Jane noticed a photograph of Dr Vodden pinned to the whiteboard. Underneath it Dixon had written 'Vodden 1979' in red ink.

'So, we have two murders, over three decades apart, and yet clearly connected. Jane and I will be focussing on that,' said Dixon.

'What's the connection then, Sir?' asked Pearce.

'We're going to be working on the basis that it's a patient or patients. Both were happily married at that time, so we can rule out personal involvement for the time being, I think. We can always come back to it later if we get nowhere. That leaves work. A doctor and a nurse. So we'll be going back through patient records to find anyone they both treated.'

'Will the records be available going back that far?' asked Harding.

'Good question, Dave,' replied Dixon. 'We'll soon find out. And we've got a copy of Dr Vodden's personnel file already, of course.'

'So we're ruling out the husband?' asked Pearce.

'We are.'

Dixon pointed to the box of papers that he had brought back from Norfolk. It was on the desk in front of him.

'Jane, Vodden's personnel file is in there.'

'Yes, Sir.'

Dixon looked at WPC Willmott.

'Christian name?'

'Louise, Sir.'

'Louise, would you help DC Winter go through that box and extract anything else that might be relevant? There's all sorts of stuff in there from the 1979 investigation. We didn't have time to go through it all in detail so just copied the lot.'

'Yes, Sir.'

'Jane, start with getting hold of Valerie Manning's NHS file. And we need Dr Vodden's patient list for each year he was in Burnham. He was at Arundel House Surgery in Love Lane.'

'Yes, Sir.'

'Right then, what else have we come up with?'

Silence.

'Nothing?'

'I'm afraid so, Sir,' said Harding. 'We've had no sightings at all on the Saturday evening from Morrisons. House to house drew a blank, too, so all we've got is the statement you took from Daniel Fisher and the CCTV footage.'

'OK,' said Dixon, 'let's go for a full reconstruction this coming Saturday. From 4 p.m. onwards. I'll liaise with DCI Lewis and get the TV cameras there. Plenty of officers handing out leaflets. The usual drill. We can have officers in Morrisons and the pubs opposite all evening, speaking to anyone and everyone.'

'Yes, Sir.'

'Let's see if we can't jog someone's memory. Can you organise that, Dave?'

Harding nodded.

'Let's assume that the murderer waited until the last minute to hide behind the bus stop. They must, at some point, have come to Morrisons to check that Valerie's car was there. Right?'

'They could have driven past before going out to Berrow Church, surely?' said Jane.

'Good point,' said Dixon. 'The jetty camera has automatic number plate recognition, doesn't it, Dave?'

'It does.'

'Then check every car that drove past it from 4 p.m. onwards.'

'Will do, Sir.'

'It's a long shot, is my guess. Any local would know the cameras are there but it's worth a try. Anything else?'

WPC Louise Willmott raised her hand.

'Yes, Louise.'

'Sorry, Sir, but if it was a patient treated by Dr Vodden before he left for Norfolk in 1976, why did he or she wait until 1979 to kill him? That's over three years.'

'That's a very good question. There could be any number of reasons for that, though, and don't forget the old saying: "Revenge is a dish best served cold".'

Dixon sat down in front of a spare computer, logged in and checked his email. Nothing of interest. He sent a message to Dave Harding asking him to email across a copy of the CCTV footage from the car park at the time Valerie Manning was abducted. Then he switched off the computer. Jane shouted to him from the other side of the CID Room. She had a phone in her right hand and was covering the microphone with her left.

'DCI Lewis is on the phone, Sir. Says he wants to see you at 10 a.m.'

Dixon looked at his watch.

'Tell him I'll be there at 11 a.m., will you?'

———⌣———

Number 17 Margaret Avenue was a double fronted red brick bungalow with new PVC windows. Dixon noticed that the bungalow next door had the original metal window frames and the paint was peeling off them, too. No doubt an estate agent would say it was in need of refreshment. Mrs Emily Townsend's was, however, immaculate. The concrete path that led to the front door was new and appeared to have been swept recently. Dixon knew from experience that keeping a front garden clear of sand anywhere near the seafront at Burnham was all but impossible. He knocked on the door and waited. A dog started barking. Dixon could hear footsteps, and a female voice telling the dog to shut up.

The door was answered by a woman in her early seventies. She had dark brown hair, obviously dyed, a round face and wore horn rimmed spectacles. A second pair hung around her neck on a string. She was dressed in a smart two piece wool suit.

'I'm looking for Mrs Emily Townsend.'

'And you are?'

'Detective Inspector Nick Dixon.'

'You'd better come in.'

Mrs Townsend stood to one side and allowed Dixon into her hall. She looked nervously up and down the road outside and was embarrassed when she realised that Dixon had noticed.

'Nosy neighbours,' she said, shrugging her shoulders.

Dixon followed her through to the kitchen at the back of the bungalow.

'Would you like a cup of coffee, Inspector?'

'Yes, thank you, that would be very kind.'

'Please sit down,' said Mrs Townsend.

Dixon sat at the kitchen table.

'I was hoping you might be able to answer a couple of questions for me.'

'Of course, but I've already given a statement to DS Harding.'

'I've read it but have a couple of other questions, if that's OK?'

'Fine.'

Mrs Townsend handed Dixon a mug of coffee and a spoon. She placed the sugar bowl on the table and then sat down opposite him.

'Your statement mentions that you were a former work colleague of Valerie's?'

'I was.'

'Are you a nurse?'

'Long since retired, Inspector. But, yes, I was a nurse. An SEN. State Enrolled Nurse. Heaven knows what they call them these days.'

'And Valerie?'

'The same.'

'Where did you work?'

'We met at Weston-super-Mare Hospital. The old one. Before they knocked it down and built the new one.'

'Which department were you in?'

'A&E. We were both in A&E.'

'When was this?'

'We met in January 1974. Started on the same day, would you believe it? Seems like a lifetime ago.'

'How long did you work together?'

'I left A&E the following year, in 1975. I moved over to geriatrics and then on to private nursing in the end. We stayed friends, of course. Val stayed in the NHS until she retired.'

'When was that?'

'Ten years ago, I suppose.'

'And was she in A&E all that time?'

'Yes, she was. She loved it.'

'What did she do? What was her job?'

'She was the triage nurse. It was her job to see patients on arrival and assess them. Urgent, can wait, go home, that sort of thing.'

'The cutting edge.'

'Very much so. The drunks were the worst. More recently it's been druggies. She was glad to retire when she did, I think.'

'Was she ever assaulted?'

'A few times. It's an occupational hazard in A&E, especially on the Saturday night shift.'

'And you?'

'Once. That's why I moved, although it wasn't much safer on a geriatric ward.'

'Did anyone ever threaten Valerie?'

'All the time. She never took it seriously. You can't, otherwise you'd go mad.'

'OK, leaving aside drunks and cranks, were there any particular cases that upset her or disturbed her? We are looking around the late seventies.'

'That's a long time ago.'

'It is.'

Emily Townsend shook her head.

'Were there any cases that she mentioned to you?' asked Dixon.

'I really can't think of anything, Inspector.'

'This really is very important, Mrs Towns . . .' Dixon's voice tailed off. He noticed that Emily Townsend was no longer listening to him. She was deep in thought. He waited.

'We went on holiday together a few years ago. A week in Marbella. It was the first and only time she mentioned it.'

Dixon waited.

'A young child. A girl. She turned her away from A&E. The child died later that same day, or maybe it was the next day. That's all I know.'

'When was this?'

'I don't really know. But I got the impression it was a long time ago.'

'What made you think that?'

'She said it had haunted her for years.'

'Did she mention the name of the child?'

'No.'

'The parents?'

'No. No names. That really is all she ever said in all the time I knew her, Inspector. Just that once. We'd had a few glasses of wine and she got a bit emotional. Had a few tears.'

'Thank you, Mrs Townsend. You've been very helpful.'

Dixon placed his card on the table.

'If you think of anything else, no matter how trivial it may seem, please telephone me straight away, will you?'

'I will.'

Dixon arrived at Bridgwater Police Station just before 11 a.m. He gave DCI Lewis a full briefing on the investigation to date, including a detailed account of the murder of Dr Vodden and its implications for the current enquiry. Lewis had expressed some concern that Dixon was focussing too much on patients as the only connection between the two victims but was content for him to pursue it for the time being.

He readily agreed to the reconstruction scheduled for the Saturday night and would set it up with the PR Officer, Vicky Thomas. Lewis' parting shot, 'Don't fuck it up', was ringing in Dixon's ears as he walked out to his Land Rover.

Dixon decided to go for a quick walk in Victoria Park before heading back to Burnham and was just letting Monty off the lead when his phone rang.

'Hi, Jane, what's up?'

'We've got another one.'

'Where?'

'A block of flats at the top of Poplar Road.'

'Where are you?'

'On my way there.'

'Wait for me before you go in. Ring Scenes of Crime and Roger Poland as well, will you?'

'Will do.'

Poplar Road led directly to the beach and was sealed off at the junction with Herbert Road by the time Dixon arrived. He could see three police cars and an ambulance parked adjacent to the block of flats. They were just behind the seating area overlooking the beach. He noticed Jane's car parked in Herbert Road, so he parked behind it. It had started to rain so he reached for his umbrella and then walked across to the waiting group of officers. Jane was sheltering under the open carport of the property opposite. He beckoned her over.

'What's the story, then?' asked Dixon.

A uniformed police constable moved forward to shelter under Dixon's umbrella and opened his notebook.

'Mr John Hawkins, Sir. He didn't turn up for his usual bridge evening at the community centre last week and when he didn't turn up last night, either, Mrs Norris decided to knock on his door, which she did an hour or so ago.'

'And?'

'When she got no reply, she opened the letterbox to look through. It was then that she dialled 999.'

'What could she see?'

'Nothing, Sir. It was the smell.'

'Anyone been in there yet?'

'Only me,' said the police officer. 'It's not a pretty sight.'

'Scenes of Crime and the pathologist on their way?'

'Yes,' said Jane.

'Come on, then, Constable Winter. Let's get this over with.'

Dixon looked at the police officer.

'Flat 21, Sir. PC Jones is at the bottom of the stairs and will show you up. PC Heath is on the door.'

'Thank you.'

Seaview was a block of flats familiar to Dixon. It had been built on the seafront adjacent to the beach, with each flat facing directly out to sea. Many years before, its front garden had been his shortcut into town when the tide was in. It was constructed of grey stone, or at least had been clad in grey stone, and had been built in three connected blocks, each containing eight flats over four floors. All of the flats had a square bay window at the front facing directly out to sea. A view to die for.

Dixon looked along the back of Seaview and could see three entrances. Flat 21 was in the third block along. PC Jones was standing at the entrance, sheltering as best he could from the rain. Dixon and Jane showed their warrant cards.

'Third floor, Sir. PC Heath will show you in.'

'What about the other residents?'

'They've been asked to stay indoors.'

Dixon noticed the smell before he reached the first floor. It was unmistakable. John Hawkins had clearly been dead for some time. They arrived on the third floor to find PC Heath standing next to the door to flat 21. It was open.

'Keep the bloody door shut, Constable,' said Dixon. He pointed to a window on the landing, 'and for heaven's sake, open that window.'

Dixon turned to Jane.

'You got any gloves?'

Jane reached into her handbag and produced two pairs of disposable rubber gloves. She passed one pair to Dixon and put the other on.

'This is not going to be pleasant.'

Jane nodded. She was holding her breath and couldn't speak.

Dixon stepped forward into the doorway of the flat. The full horror of the smell hit him. He turned away. Jane began to retch.

Dixon reached into his pocket and produced a handful of black plastic bags. He split them into two bundles, placed one over his nose and mouth and then handed the other to Jane. She put them in her right hand and clamped them over her nose and mouth. She looked quizzically at Dixon.

'Scented dog bags.'

Dixon walked along the hallway and into the lounge. He opened the windows at the front of the flat. He stood for a moment in front of the open window, taking in the fresh air, before replacing the bags over his nose and mouth. He then stepped to one side to allow Jane some fresh air.

The room was tidy. It contained a three seat sofa and two armchairs arranged around a pine coffee table. There were two empty wine glasses on the table. An artificial fireplace had been bolted to the wall and in the back corner of the room was a small pine dining table and chairs. A laptop computer was open on the table. A doorway led through into the kitchen. There was an open bottle of red wine on the side. Dixon had been a police officer long enough to know that the bottle was half empty rather than half full.

He walked back into the lounge. Jane was still standing in front of the open window. He could see her chest heaving with each deep gulp of fresh air. Dixon touched the radiator. It was on. That would explain the powerful smell.

He retraced his steps back to the hallway and followed the passage to the rear of the flat. The door to the master bedroom was closed. He took several shallow breaths and then ensured that his dog bags were forming a tight seal around his nose and mouth. Then he opened the door.

He had known what to expect, but that had not prepared him for the full horror of the scene that lay before him. The headless body of the late John Hawkins lay on the double bed, which now had the appearance of summer fruit pudding. He was naked and the process of decomposition was well advanced. His skin was a hideous patchwork of black, blue and yellow. The blood on the pillow and mattress had congealed into a dark red sickly sweet crust.

Dixon noticed a single stab wound to the left side of John Hawkins' chest. If it had been the same knife used to kill Valerie Manning then the blade would certainly have penetrated the heart, killing him instantly. The head had been severed halfway up the neck. There appeared to be very little blood spatter up the walls or on the headboard, which told Dixon that John Hawkins' heart had stopped beating before he was decapitated.

Dixon looked around the room. There were built in wardrobes either side of the bed and a chest of drawers against the wall behind him. Opposite the end of the bed was a dressing table and to the right of that, in the corner of the room, was a sink.

Dixon walked around the end of the bed to look out of the window. Only then did he notice the severed head of John Hawkins in the sink. It was lying on its side, facing the taps. Dixon leaned over to check the eyes. They were closed and the facial expression was calm. John Hawkins had not known what was happening to him.

Jane appeared in the doorway of the bedroom. Dixon spoke through the dog bags clamped over his mouth with his right hand.

'Single stab wound to the heart. Then the head was severed. I don't envy Roger Poland this one.'

'Where is it?' asked Jane.

'In the sink.'

It again.

Jane stepped forward to look in the sink. The discolouration of the skin was less noticeable through John Hawkins' thick grey hair and beard. She turned to Dixon.

'He looks almost calm.'

'He does. Pop outside, will you, and find out when Poland and the scenes of crime team will get here.'

Jane did not need to be asked twice. Dixon moved back through to the lounge and stood in front of the open window to get some fresh air. He replaced his makeshift mask over his mouth and turned to examine the lounge more closely. He noticed a pile of letters that had been opened and replaced in their envelopes. He picked up the letters from the dining table and then returned to the relative safety of the open window to go through them one by one.

The correspondence was routine. John Hawkins was methodical in his approach, each letter having been opened, read and then replaced in the envelope. Dixon found gas, water and electricity bills, all paid by direct debit. There was also a bank statement and two letters dealing with a forthcoming hospital appointment. There were several birthday cards, one containing a letter from his sister, a credit card bill and a letter from the Department for Work and Pensions dealing with his Winter Fuel Payment.

The last envelope in the pile contained what Dixon had been looking for. It was a payslip for the October payment of John Hawkins' occupational pension. And it came from NHS Pensions.

Dixon replaced the pile of letters on the dining room table, having kept the pension slip, and went outside to find Jane. He could see that two Scientific Services vans had arrived and Jane was briefing the senior scenes of crime officer, Watson. Dixon retrieved his umbrella from PC Jones and walked over to them.

'Sounds grim,' said Watson.

'It is,' replied Dixon. 'Looks to me as if he was killed before Valerie Manning and he's been in there with the central heating on for at least a week.'

Watson turned to address his team, who were unloading equipment from the backs of the vans.

'Masks, everybody.'

'There are two wine glasses on the coffee table, so it looks like he had company, and a computer on the dining table that'll need to go to High Tech.'

'Leave it to us,' replied Watson.

'What about Roger Poland?' asked Dixon, turning to Jane.

'Ten minutes. He's on his way.'

'I'll hang on for him. There's something I need you to do, Jane.'

'What?'

'How far have you got with Valerie Manning's personnel file?'

'The NHS Trust Records Office assured me I would have it by the end of tomorrow.'

'What about Vodden's patient lists?'

'Same.'

'Not good enough. Yell and scream at them if you have to, but we must have those lists by the end of today.'

'OK.'

'We'll also need John Hawkins' NHS file.'

'He worked for the NHS?'

'He did.'

Dixon handed the NHS Pension pay slip to Jane.

'That can't be a coincidence, can it?'

'We're on the right track, all right,' said Dixon.

'Is there something you're not telling me?'

'Just get those patient lists, Jane. I'll catch up with you later.'

Dixon watched Jane walk down Poplar Road towards her car. She went round the corner into Herbert Road and out of sight just as Dr Poland turned off Berrow Road into Poplar Road at the far end. He drove up to the police cordon at the junction of Poplar Road and Herbert Road and was allowed through. He parked behind the Scientific Services vans. Dixon walked over to meet him.

⌣

'Jane Winter said this one's pretty grim.'

'He's been dead for anything up to two weeks and the central heating has been on in there.'

'Well, I haven't had my lunch yet.'

'Good job.'

Roger Poland went round to the boot of his car and took out his bag. He then followed Dixon over to the communal entrance of the block of flats. Once in the hallway, he put on a set of disposable overalls and a facemask. He handed a spare mask to Dixon and then they walked up the stairs to flat 21.

There were already four scenes of crime officers at work in the flat and Dixon could see camera flashes coming from both the lounge and the rear bedroom. He gestured towards the bedroom at the rear of the flat.

'The body's in there.'

Dixon stood behind Roger Poland as he examined the body. Dr Poland looked first at John Hawkins' body and then at his severed head in the sink. He took no more than a couple of minutes before gesturing to Dixon to follow him outside. They stood by the open window on the landing at the top of the communal stairway.

'I thought you'd appreciate the fresh air.'

'Thank you,' replied Dixon.

'Have you spotted the stab wound to the heart?'

'Yes.'

'Looks like the same knife and it was probably the fatal wound. Judging by the blood pattern, the head was severed post mortem and it looks like an electric knife again. I'll need to look at him under the microscope to confirm that, though.'

'How long?'

'At least a week, possibly longer. I'll need to check the central heating settings. I'll let you know soon as I can.'

'Good. I'll leave you to it, if I may.'

Dixon walked towards the top of the stairs.

'We still haven't had that beer,' said Poland.

'No, we must do that,' replied Dixon. 'We must do that.'

Dixon knocked on the door of 7 Manor Drive just after 3 p.m. The door was answered by Peter Manning.

'Do you have any news, Inspector?'

'We're working on it, Mr Manning. I do have a couple of questions that I need to ask you, if you can spare me a few minutes?'

'Yes, of course. Come in.'

Dixon followed Peter Manning through to the lounge. Manning sat in the armchair by the fireplace and Dixon sat on the sofa.

'Fire away,' said Peter Manning.

'How long did you know Mrs Manning?'

'We met in 1972 and married in 1974.'

'That was when she moved to Weston-super-Mare Hospital?' asked Dixon.

'Yes. She moved down here when we got married. She was at Frenchay Hospital in Bristol before that.'

'What did she do at the hospital?'

'She was the triage nurse in A&E.'

'And that involved?'

'It was her job to make the first assessment of a patient when they arrived. Being at the sharp end, she called it. And she loved it.'

'Stressful, I'd imagine?'

'Yes, it was, and sometimes dangerous. I begged her to do something else but she wouldn't.'

'Do you ever remember her getting it wrong?'

'What's that supposed to mean?'

'Making the wrong assessment of a patient, perhaps, and treating them as not urgent when they should have been urgent?'

'You don't seriously think . . .'

'It's one line of enquiry, Mr Manning. Please, can you think of any . . .'

'There was one case, I remember. Years ago.'

'Involving a child?' asked Dixon.

'Yes. It was a little girl. She died.'

'Can you remember her name?'

'No. Val thought she had flu and sent her home.'

'What happened?'

'The child died the next day. Turned out it was meningitis.'

'And you can't remember the name?'

'I'm sorry.'

'Was there an inquest?'

'Yes. Val had to give a statement.'

'Did you go to the inquest?'

'No, she wouldn't let me.'

'When was this?'

'Not long after we got married. So, say, 1974 or 1975.'

'What happened after the inquest?'

'Nothing, as far as I know. She never mentioned it again. You don't seriously think this has anything to do with her murder?'

'I really don't know, Mr Manning, but I can assure you I will find out.'

Dixon sat in his Land Rover and rang Jane.

'What news on Vodden's patient lists, Jane?'

'He was at Arundel House Surgery from August 1971 to March 1976. They've promised to fax the lists to me this afternoon. First of January in each year.'

'Good. Let me know soon as they arrive and run me off a few spare copies of '74, '75 and '76, will you?'

'Will do.'

'See you later,' said Dixon, ringing off.

Chapter Six

It was just before 4 p.m. when Dixon parked across the entrance to the Shire Hall in Taunton, a magnificent grey stone Gothic building with stone parapets and turrets. Once the council offices, it was now the Taunton Crown Court and the venue for inquests held by the West Somerset coroner. A security guard spotted him straight away.

'You can't leave that there.'

Dixon produced his warrant card.

'I'll be back in ten minutes. Keep an eye on it, will you?'

The security guard allowed him through the checkpoint.

'Where will I find the coroner?'

'Up the stairs, turn right. He's sitting in court one.'

'Thanks.'

Dixon ran up the stairs. He slowed to a walking pace as he arrived at the door to court one. He opened the door quietly, stepped inside and allowed it to close behind him. The West Somerset coroner, Michael Roseland, was hearing an inquest into the death of a man killed in a jet skiing accident off Burnham-on-Sea. A solicitor was cross-examining a witness. The court usher looked up. Dixon waved to him and gestured outside. The usher understood the message and followed Dixon back out onto the landing.

Dixon produced his warrant card again.

'I need to speak to the coroner urgently.'

'He's hearing an inquest . . . we are not splitting a word here.'

'I am investigating a triple murder and I need to speak to him now. Ask him to adjourn for five minutes. That's all I need.'

The court usher looked again at Dixon's warrant card.

'He finishes for the afternoon in half an hour.'

'Now, please.'

'Follow me.'

Dixon followed the usher into court one and waited at the back. He watched the usher approach the coroner and whisper in his right ear. The coroner reached forward and placed his left hand over the microphone on the front of his desk. The coroner looked at Dixon and then back to the usher.

'Ladies and Gentlemen, I'm afraid that an urgent matter has come up. There will be a short adjournment. No more than five minutes, I'm told.'

The coroner stood up.

'All rise,' said the usher. All present stood up. They then turned and looked at Dixon.

The coroner left the court through a door behind the bench. The usher walked over to Dixon and escorted him out of the court and along the landing. A locked door led through to a long corridor.

'This had better be good. He's not happy about this. At all.'

Dixon ignored him.

The usher stopped outside a large carved oak door.

'Here you go,' he said, opening the door.

'Detective Inspector Dixon, Sir.'

'Thank you, James. I'll buzz when I'm ready to go back in.'

'This won't take long, Sir', said Dixon.

The usher left the room.

'Now, what's this all about, Inspector?'

'I'm investigating a triple murder, Sir. I've got three people who have had their heads cut off. Two within the last few days, one in 1979.'

'Good heavens.'

'I need access to inquest records going back to the mid-seventies. They are held at the Somerset Archive and I need your written permission, I'm told, Sir.'

'Well, that's easily done.'

The coroner opened the top drawer of his desk and took out a piece of paper. He read aloud as he wrote.

'I hereby authorise Detective Inspector Dixon to have access to all inquest records that he may require . . .'

'And to keep copies, please, Sir.'

'. . . and to take copies thereof. Signed, Michael Roseland, West Somerset Coroner.'

He handed the letter to Dixon.

'Do you need anything else, Inspector?'

'No, Sir. Thank you.'

'I expect I'll be finding out about all this in due course?'

'You will, Sir.'

Dixon was on his way to the door.

'And good luck to you.'

'Thank you, Sir.'

Dixon arrived at the Somerset Heritage Centre just before 4.30 p.m. A large purpose built complex on the outskirts of Taunton, it housed the entire Somerset document and photographic archive. He presented his warrant card to the receptionist.

'I need access to inquest records from the mid-seventies, please. And I need it urgently.'

'We don't accept document requests within an hour of closing and we close at 5 p.m.'

Dixon took a deep breath. He noticed a CCTV camera above the reception desk and resolved to remain calm.

'Is there a manager available who might be able to help me?'

He watched the receptionist look at the clock on the wall.

'It is rather urgent,' he said.

She sighed and picked up the telephone. 'Inquest records are held in the document archive. I'll see if the document manager is available.'

Dixon paced up and down in the reception area.

'She's on her way,' said the receptionist.

A few moments later a door opened opposite the reception desk.

'Are you the police officer?'

'Yes. Detective Inspector Nick Dixon.'

'My name is Rachel Smerdon. I'm the document manager.'

She was in her early twenties with dark brown shoulder length hair. She wore dark trousers and a white blouse.

'Is there anywhere we can have a chat?' asked Dixon.

'There's an interview room through here,' said Rachel, gesturing towards the door.

Once in the interview room, Dixon showed her his warrant card.

'I am investigating three murders. I'll spare you the gory details. Two are recent and one took place in 1979. They are connected by the death of a child that took place sometime between 1974 and 1976. Possibly 1979 but we'll start with 1976. My understanding is that one of the murder victims gave evidence at the child's inquest.'

'That's easy. What was the child's name?'

'I don't know.'

'That's not so easy.'

'I thought not. It's possible I might be able to come up with a name, or at least narrow it down. But otherwise, I need to look at every file until I find the right one.'

'You'll need the coroner's permission.'

Dixon handed her the letter from Michael Roseland.

'Our records are not computerised that far back. It'll be the old index cards.'

'What about the files? Are they held together?'

'Yes. In archive boxes.'

'And the index cards. What information is on them?'

'I'll need to have a look. It'll be name, date of death and verdict, certainly. Possibly date of birth but I'll need to check.'

'How many boxes of files are there?'

'Loads.'

'Will you be able to get them out for me?'

'The index cards?'

'And the files.'

'But you don't know which ones.'

'All of them.'

'Bloody hell.'

'It's good old fashioned police work. I'll be back first thing in the morning with some help and we'll keep looking until we find the one we're searching for.'

'Yes, I can get the files out for you, but it's not going to be easy.'

'What time do you open in the morning?'

'At 9 a.m but I can be here from 7 a.m. I'll make a start on the files.'

'Can I have your mobile number, Rachel? If I can narrow it down overnight, it will save you getting all of them out.'

Dixon exchanged phone numbers with Rachel and they agreed to meet back at the Somerset Heritage Centre at 7 a.m the following morning. Rachel gave Dixon directions to the staff entrance at the rear of the building.

Dixon sat in his Land Rover and rang Jane.

'Have you got Vodden's patient lists, Jane?

'Yes.'

'What about Valerie's personnel file?'

'That too.'

'Anything interesting?'

'Not really.'

'OK. I'm on my way home now. Shall I pick up a Chinese?'

'Where are you?'

'Taunton.'

'What are you doing there?'

'I'll tell you later. Do you want a takeaway?'

'Yes. Do you want me to bring the lists?'

'Yes, please. It's going to be a long night.'

Dixon was home just before 6.30 p.m. There was a note sticking out of his letterbox.

'In the Red Cow. Jane.'

He put the Chinese takeaway in the oven to keep it warm and then walked across to the pub with Monty. Jane was sitting at the bar with a drink.

'This is ridiculous. We must get you a key,' said Dixon.

'A key? Things must be getting serious,' replied Jane. 'Where's the food?'

'In the oven. I've got time for a beer.'

Dixon ordered himself a pint and they sat at a table in the far corner of the bar.

'What's the story, then?' asked Jane.

'I went to see Emily Townsend.'

'The friend who dropped Valerie off at Morrisons car park?'

'That's right. Friend and . . .' Dixon paused, '. . . former work colleague.'

'Shit. She was, wasn't she?'

'They started in the A&E at Weston on the same day in 1974 and had been friends ever since.'

'Well?'

'Emily couldn't hack it in A&E and moved on to geriatrics, I think she said. Valerie stayed in A&E. She was the triage nurse. She would make the initial assessment when a patient first arrived. She only ever mentioned this once to Emily. They were on holiday and Valerie had had a few glasses of wine, but she said that she'd got it wrong once, in the early days, and had turned away a child who later died.'

'A patient of Dr Vodden's?'

'That remains to be seen. I've confirmed it with Peter Manning who remembers Valerie giving evidence at an inquest not long after they got married. He thought it was 1975. They married in 1974.'

'And no one can remember a name, I suppose?'

'That'd be too easy,' replied Dixon. 'I was hoping there'd be a copy of the statement Valerie gave to the inquest on her file.'

'No such luck. So, where have you been?'

'To see the coroner and then to the Somerset document archive. The document manager will be getting all of the inquest files out for us in the morning and we'll go through each one until we find the file we're looking for.'

'That could take days,' said Jane.

'Not if we can find an infant in Dr Vodden's patient lists who dies.'

'How do we do that?'

'We check his patient lists for anyone named as a patient of his on 1st January 1974 but who was not listed on 1st January 1976. There will be some who have moved away, some who died and some who changed doctor. But it narrows it down, doesn't it?'

'Have you seen these lists?'

'No.'

'They're huge.'

'Drink up, then. It's going to be a longer night than I thought.'

—⏜—

Dixon looked at Dr Vodden's patient list for 1st January 1974. It gave patient name, National Health Service number, date of birth and address for eight hundred and fifty-one patients.

'Here's what we're going to do. You look at the January 1975 list and I'll read out the name of any patient on my list born after 1st January 1964. We are looking for any child whose name is on this list but not on your list. OK?'

'Yes.'

'Then we repeat the process with the 1975 and 1976 lists.'

'OK.'

'We should end up with a list of names of children who, for whatever reason, ceased to be a patient of Dr Vodden's in either 1974 or 1975. If needs be, we can go through the other lists tomorrow.'

Dixon began looking down the list of patients.

'Here we go. Adams, Simon John. Born 2nd December 1966.'

'Still on the list,' said Jane.

'Still alive on 1st January 1975 then,' replied Dixon.

By midnight they had finished comparing the 1974 list to the 1975 list. Dixon looked at the list of names he had written on the back of his gas bill.

'Thirteen. All of whom either died, changed doctor or moved away in 1974.'

'That's a lot, isn't it?'

'I don't know if it's a lot or not. But, don't forget, there was a boarding school in Burnham back then, so some of them may have been pupils there.'

'That might explain it,' replied Jane.

Dixon began reading out names from the 1975 list. Jane compared them with the 1976 list and by 1 a.m. they had added another ten names to the list.

'Time for bed,' said Dixon.

——— ———

By 7 a.m., Dixon and Jane were waiting outside the staff entrance at the Somerset Heritage Centre. The car park was otherwise empty. Dixon had sent Rachel Smerdon a text message to let her know that they had narrowed it down to a list of twenty-three names. She had replied saying she was on her way.

A few minutes later, a black Ford Ka turned into the car park and pulled into the space next to Dixon's Land Rover.

Dixon made the introductions.

'You've had a long night, then,' said Rachel.

'It didn't take as long as I thought it would,' replied Dixon, 'but we've only checked two years. The most likely ones, based on what we know so far.'

Rachel showed them through to her office. She switched on the coffee machine. Dixon handed her the list of names.

'This is a list of twenty-three children who ceased to be patients of Dr Ralph Vodden in either 1974 or 1975. Some will have moved away or changed doctor but some will have died. And I'm hoping at least one will have been the subject of an inquest.'

'Help yourselves,' said Rachel, gesturing to the coffee machine. 'I'll go and see what I can find. It might take a while, though.' She closed the door behind her.

'What if she doesn't find anything?' asked Jane.

'She'll find something. And if she doesn't, we widen the search.'

Dixon picked up a copy of the *Somerset County Gazette* and pretended to read it. Jane closed her eyes and pretended to be asleep. It was not a conversation either of them wished to pursue.

It was nearly twenty minutes later when Rachel Smerdon reappeared. She was carrying three files, each of them light brown and perhaps an inch thick. She handed them to Dixon.

'Here you go, Inspector. Three. I wasn't expecting to find any, to be honest.'

'We're going to need to read through these quite carefully . . .'

'That's OK. I'll leave you to it. Ring me on my mobile when you've finished.'

Dixon handed the top file to Jane. He then looked at the next on the pile.

It belonged to Rosemary Claire Southall. The label on the cover gave a date of birth of 25th March 1972 and a date of death of 17th September 1974. Aged two and a half, thought Dixon. The inquest took place on 11th February 1975. The cause of death was given as 1(a) meningitis and the coroner had recorded a narrative verdict.

Dixon had found the file he was looking for.

He opened it. The first document was the coroner's verdict. Dixon knew that a narrative verdict was reserved for those rare cases requiring further explanation or comment from the coroner, above and beyond the usual accident, natural causes, open or misadventure verdicts.

He read aloud.

'Cause of death 1(a) meningitis. Verdict . . . natural causes . . . contributed to by neglect and/or lack of care . . . gross failings . . . failed to realise significance of vital signs . . . should not have discharged . . . gross failure to refer . . .'

Jane stopped reading and looked up.

'That sounds like it.'

'It does. Let's have a look at the witness statements, shall we?'

Dixon leafed through the documents in the file. He extracted a statement from the file and banged it down on the desk.

'Dr Ralph Vodden. I am a general practitioner . . .'

He banged a second statement on the desk.

'Valerie Manning. I am a nurse employed in the accident and emergency department . . .'

Then another.

'John Hawkins. I am an ambulance paramedic . . .'

He stopped.

'Bloody hell.'

'What?'

Jane waited.

'What?'

'There are two more.'

'Who?'

'Sandra Gibson. Receptionist at Arundel House Surgery.'

Dixon began reading the statement.

'And?' asked Jane.

Dixon turned back to the other statements.

'Mr Julian Spalding FRCS, consultant paediatrician at Weston-super-Mare Hospital.'

'What happened to them, I wonder?'

'We need to find out pretty damn quick. What's the time?'

'Nearly eight,' replied Jane.

'I want a briefing at 9 a.m. See if you can get Lewis there too.'

Jane rang Dave Harding while Dixon rang Rachel Smerdon. He could hear her phone ringing in the corridor outside and she opened the door to her office without answering it.

'Found what you were looking for?' she asked.

Dixon disconnected the call.

'Yes. I'm going to need to take this file, Rachel.'

'I can't let it go, but you can copy it.'

'No time, I'm afraid.'

'But . . .'

'Did you read about that woman who was beheaded last Saturday?'

'Yes. Don't tell me it's . . .'

'We found another one yesterday.'

Rachel opened her mouth to speak but said nothing.

'They both gave evidence at this inquest,' said Dixon, pointing to the file. 'As did two other people who may still be alive. We have to find them and I don't have time to waste photocopying.'

'Take it,' replied Rachel.

<hr />

Dixon and Jane headed north on the M5. It was just after 8 a.m. on a dull and overcast November morning. Jane was driving Dixon's Land Rover. He was sitting in the passenger seat, reading Rosie Southall's inquest file.

They arrived at Burnham-on-Sea Police Station just before 8.30 a.m. Jane left Dixon sitting in the passenger seat and went into the station. He was still reading when there was loud tap on the passenger window. It was DCI Lewis. Dixon got out the car.

'This had better be good, Nick.'

<hr />

The briefing began at 9 a.m. sharp.

'Rosie Southall. Died 17th September 1974. Aged two and a half. The inquest took place in February 1975. This is the file,' said Dixon, holding it up. 'The cause of death was meningitis. The coroner recorded a verdict of natural causes contributed to by neglect and/or lack of care on the part of the medical staff who attended her. In other words, she died due to medical negligence.'

'And Dr Vodden and Valerie Manning were among the medical staff?' asked Lewis.

'They were. And so was John Hawkins.'

'That comes in the major breakthrough category.'

'It does, Mark,' said Dixon. 'It's a long story but I'll keep it short.' He poured himself a drink from the water tower. 'The statement from the mother, Frances Southall, gives the overall picture of what happened. Frances was concerned about her daughter on the morning of 16th September. Rosie had a high temperature and was having difficulty breathing. So, she took Rosie to see her doctor.'

'Ralph Vodden at Arundel House Surgery?'

'That's right, Dave. He says in his statement that he thought it was nothing serious and sent her home. He told Frances to give her Calpol, apparently.'

'Was Calpol available then?' asked Jane.

'I suppose it must have been,' replied Dixon. 'Anyway, Rosie's condition deteriorated throughout the day so Frances took her back to see Vodden around 3 p.m. He was out on home visits and the receptionist, Sandra Gibson, refused to let her see another doctor. She told Frances to take Rosie home and put her to bed.'

'The receptionist said that?' asked Lewis.

'Yes, Sir.'

Lewis shook his head. Dixon continued.

'The father arrived home at 6 p.m. Rosie was still no better so he called an ambulance. Enter John Hawkins, who took them to the A&E at Weston-super-Mare hospital.'

'Where they met Valerie Manning?'

'Yes, Dave.'

'You can just see it coming, can't you?'

'Sadly, you can,' replied Dixon. 'Valerie thought Rosie was suffering from flu. The consultant paediatrician, Mr Julian Spalding, was consulted but, based on Valerie's assessment, he refused to see them. So, Valerie sent them home. By midnight, Rosie's condition was such that her father, David, called an ambulance for the second time. Unfortunately, it was manned by John Hawkins, and he refused to take them to the hospital again. He accused them of time wasting, according to Frances Southall's statement.'

'Time wasting?'

'Yes, Jane.'

'What happened next?' asked Lewis.

'Rosie Southall died in her mother's arms at 5 a.m. that morning.'

Dixon looked around the room. Silence. There were tears streaming down Louise Willmott's cheeks.

'Sorry, Sir. I have a two year old girl at home.'

'OK, everyone, what's done is done. Let's get on with sorting this mess out, shall we?'

'Yes, Sir,' said Mark Pearce.

'Let's assume Rosie's father, David Southall, is killing them for revenge . . .'

'You could hardly blame him.'

'C'mon, Mark, you know the score. We can't allow that sort of sentiment to creep in.'

'No, Sir.'

'So, we come back to your question, Louise.'

'Mine?'

'Yes. Why the gaps? Three years before the murder of Dr Vodden and over thirty years since then. And what's the significance of the decapitation?'

'Does it have to be significant?' asked Pearce.

'Yes, it does, Mark. It's too much of a statement for it not to be. First things first, though. We have two inquest witnesses unaccounted for. Dave, I want you to drop everything and find Mr Spalding, the paediatrician.'

'Yes, Sir.'

'He's probably retired by now, so try the Department for Work and Pensions, NHS Pensions and the Royal College of Surgeons.'

Dave Harding was making notes.

'And the usual, of course, electoral roll, council tax, HM Inspector of Taxes. When you find him, take him into protective custody. Any objections, let me know.'

Dixon turned to Mark Pearce.

'Mark, I want you to find the receptionist, Sandra Gibson. Louise, will you help him, please?'

'Yes, Sir,' replied Louise Willmott.

'Find her and take her into protective custody. And don't take any crap.'

'And what are you going to do?' asked Lewis.

'Jane and I will be going after Rosie's parents.'

'What about the reconstruction scheduled for Saturday night?'

'We'll go ahead with that. I want the killer to think we are still stumbling around in the dark. As far as the outside world is concerned, we have no leads whatsoever. Right?'

'We need to release a statement about John Hawkins,' said Lewis.

'Has anyone told his next of kin? I found a birthday card from his sister.'

'Yes, Sir,' said Louise Willmott. 'She lives in Canada. She's coming over.'

'Then we can release his name and that the family have been informed. I'd rather no mention was made of his former occupation. Just that he was retired.'

'Vicky Thomas won't like that. We'll look like a bunch of idiots.'

'Yes, Sir. But we know different,' replied Dixon. 'Right then, everyone clear what they have to do? Any developments, let me know straight away. Otherwise, meet back here at 6 p.m.'

DCI Lewis gestured to Dixon to follow him outside. They met on the landing outside the CID room.

'I can tell the chief super we should have a result by the end of the day, then?'

'I wouldn't tell him that, Sir. We are closing in. We are very close even, but there's still a long way to go.'

'What do you mean?'

'There are too many unanswered questions.'

'Such as?'

'If it was Rosie's father who killed Dr Vodden, why did he wait over thirty years before killing Valerie Manning and John Hawkins?'

'There could be . . .'

'We have to find him too, don't forget.'

'Yes, but . . .'

'Tell him we are close and have made a major breakthrough. But we are still some way from wrapping this up, Sir.'

'OK, Nick. I get the message. Keep me posted.'

Lewis turned to go down the stairs.

'And well done.'

'Thank you, Sir.'

'Right then, Jane. We'll start with the father. David Southall. Find him. Concentrate on the DWP.'

'What about the electoral roll and council tax?'

'My guess is that he will have changed his name. Try them, by all means, but I expect you'll draw a blank.'

'How do you know he's changed his name?'

'I don't. But I would if I'd just decapitated my daughter's doctor. Wouldn't you?'

'I suppose I would.'

'You can change your name easily enough, but you can't change your National Insurance number.'

'They're always painfully slow, though.'

'You have my permission to scream and shout at them, if you have to.'

Dixon was putting on his coat.

'Where are you going?'

'Arundel House Surgery.'

———

Dixon waited until he had no queue behind him and the reception area was quiet. He produced his warrant card and showed it to the receptionist.

'I'd like to speak to the practice manager, please.'

'She's in a meeting.'

Dixon was not in the mood for an obstructive doctor's receptionist. A picture flashed across his mind. It was of Frances Southall, with a dying Rosie in her arms, being turned away at the same surgery.

'This is a murder enquiry and time is short. I suggest you go and get her out of whatever meeting it is. Now.'

The receptionist sighed.

'Unless you want to be arrested for obstruction.'

The receptionist got up and left the room through a door behind her desk. Dixon paced up and down in the waiting area. He noticed a plaque on the wall commemorating the opening of the new surgery by the Mayor of Burnham on 31st July 2001. The building was octagonal in shape, with the doctor's surgeries and other treatment rooms arranged around the central reception and waiting area. It was timber framed—Dixon thought it oak—and glass. At least it was not the same reception that Frances Southall had been turned away from.

'Detective Inspector?'

Dixon turned to find himself looking at a woman in her early fifties. She had short blonde hair and wore a two piece tartan trouser suit with a cream blouse. She was in a wheelchair.

'Yes, Detective Inspector Nick Dixon.' He produced his warrant card.

'I'm Lorna Campbell, the practice manager. Come through to my office.'

Dixon followed her around the octagonal reception desk to an office at the rear.

'Do sit down.'

Dixon sat in the chair in front of Lorna Campbell's desk.

'How can I help?' she asked.

'I need to track down a patient of this surgery in the mid to late seventies. Is that going to be possible?'

'Does this have anything to do with the death of John Hawkins?' Dixon hesitated.

'He was a patient here,' said Lorna Campbell.

'Yes, it does.'

'We only keep records here for current patients, I'm afraid. If they move away or change doctor, the records go to the new doctor.'

'And if they die?'

'They go to the NHS records department.'

'Do you have a record of where a patient's records might have been sent, and when?'

'It's all on computer these days, but back then it was index cards. We went over to computer records in 1997.'

'And where are the index cards now?'

'We sent them to the NHS records department when we moved to the new surgery, I'm afraid. They should still have them.'

'What about the doctors themselves?'

'What do you mean?'

'Are there any still here who were practising here in the seventies?'

'Not now. Dr Stevenson is the senior partner and he joined the practice in the early eighties, I think.'

'Can you ask him if any of the senior partners from the seventies are still alive, please?'

Lorna Campbell picked up her phone and dialled a three digit extension number.

'Richard, I've got a police officer with me. He wants to know if any doctors who practised here in the mid-seventies are still alive.'

She began making notes on the pad in front of her.

'Thanks.' She put the phone down.

'You're in luck, Inspector. Dr Eric Maunder. Retired in 2001 when we moved to this surgery. He lives at Wedmore.'

She handed Dixon the note.

'Thank you,' said Dixon. He got up to leave.

'Apologise to your receptionist for me. I may have been a bit brusque.'

Dixon was sitting in his Land Rover, watching the rain pouring down his windscreen. He looked at his watch. 10.35 a.m.

He knew he was missing something. It was there, somewhere in the documents. But was it in Dr Vodden's file or in Rosie's inquest file? He didn't know. He closed his eyes and listened to the rain hitting the roof of his car. It was a disconcerting feeling, much like recognising an actor but not remembering their name or what film they had been in.

He decided to drive to Wedmore to see Dr Maunder. He turned out of the car park and drove along the Berrow Road. His phone rang, so he pulled into the car park of the Dunstan House Hotel.

'Dixon.'

'Mark Pearce, Sir.'

'What's up, Mark?'

'Sandra Gibson, the receptionist. She married an Australian and emigrated in 1978. Went to live in Brisbane, apparently.'

'Anything else?'

'No, Sir.'

'Get onto Brisbane Police and see if she's known to them.'

'Will do.'

'What was her married name?'

'Docherty.'

'Give them both names and see what they come up with. Let me know straight away.'

'Yes, Sir.'

'Put Jane on, will you?'

Dixon could hear muffled voices.

'Hello?'

'Jane, anything from the DWP?'

'They have a National Insurance number for David Southall. Nothing for the wife. They're digging out whatever they've got and will come back to me as soon as they can.'

'Good. See you later.'

Dixon rang off. He sat in his car and watched the rain for several more minutes before he put his phone back in his coat pocket. He started the engine and then immediately switched it off again.

'Idiot!' he shouted, hitting his forehead with the palm of his right hand.

Monty woke up and started barking in the back of the Land Rover. Dixon reached for his phone and dialled Jane. He got out of his car and paced up and down in the rain.

'Have you got Vodden's patient lists there, the ones we looked at last night?'

'Give me a minute.'

Dixon could hear paper rustling.

'1974, '75 and '76?'

'Yes.'

'Got them. What's up?'

'Look at the 1974 list and turn to Rosie Southall's entry.'

Dixon could hear more paper rustling.

'Yes.'

'What's the name above it?'

'Frances Anne Southall.'

'Now look at the 1975 list. Rosie's name has gone, right?'

'Yes.'

'But Frances Southall's is still there?'

'It is.'

'OK, now look at the '76 list.'

'Give me a second.'

Dixon could feel his pulse racing. He waited.

'She's gone.'

'That's it. Thanks, Jane. Better go. Keep me posted.'

'Hang on. Is she dead?'

'She is, which explains your 'nothing for the wife' from the DWP.'

Dixon rang off. He then rang Rachel Smerdon at the Somerset Archive.

'Rachel, it's Nick Dixon.'

'How can I help, Inspector?'

'I need you to check for another inquest file. 1975 or 1976. The name of Frances Anne Southall.'

'Give me ten minutes. I'll call you back.'

Dixon left his car in the Dunstan House car park and walked around the corner into Manor Gardens. He let Monty off the lead and stood under a tree to shelter from the rain. He watched Monty and waited. Fifteen minutes later his phone rang.

'I've got an inquest file in my hand, Inspector. Frances Anne Southall died on 21st October 1975. The inquest took place on 12th April 1976. Verdict suicide.'

'I'm on my way, Rachel.'

⌣‾‾‾⌣

Dixon sat in his Land Rover in the staff car park at the Somerset Heritage Centre and opened Frances Southall's inquest file. He turned first to the coroner's findings of fact.

She had died at the Hotel Senator in Marbella, where she had been staying with her husband in a room on the fourth floor. She had attached a rope to a radiator, placed the other end around her neck and then jumped from the balcony. The cause of death was given as 1(a) hanging. Despite the absence of a suicide note, the coroner had been satisfied that Frances Southall's state of mind at the material time was depressed and/or suicidal. He therefore recorded a verdict of suicide. He expressed great sadness at her death, which he said had been caused either in whole or in part by the tragic death of her daughter, Rosie, a little over a year earlier. He offered his condolences to the family and expressed the hope that they would, in time, be able to come to terms with their loss.

Dixon turned next to the post mortem report. It was a translation of the original Spanish report, which was also on the file. He found the cause of death on the final page, but had to read it several times before he was able to grasp the significance of it. He was alone in the car, but still he read aloud.

'Cause of death: 1(a) hanging and 1(b) external decapitation.'

Dixon reached for his phone and rang Jane.

'Jane, are you at your computer?'

'Yes.'

'Go to Google.'

Dixon waited.

'Yes.'

'Put in external decapitation, will you, and tell me what you get?'

'Give me a second,' said Jane. 'It doesn't make any sense. There's a Wikipedia entry for internal decapitation.'

'Click on it and read it to me.'

'Internal decapitation, atlanto-occipital dislocation, or orthopedic decapitation describes the rare medical condition in which the skull separates from the spinal column during severe head injury. This is generally fatal, since it generally involves nerve damage or severing the spinal cord. The practice of hanging relies on internal decapitation, as it creates a situation where subjects' necks are broken under their own weight. A botched hanging can result in an external decapitation . . .'

'That's enough.'

'What does it mean, then?'

'She hanged herself. Get everyone together for another briefing. I'm on my way.'

Chapter Seven

I've got Superintendent Sean Smart of Queensland Police asking to speak to the senior investigating officer, Sir.'

Dixon took his coat off and hung it over the back of Mark Pearce's chair. Pearce stood up, leaving Dixon to sit at his desk. He passed him the phone.

'Detective Inspector Dixon, Sir. Sorry to keep you waiting.'

'That's all right, Inspector. I prefer first names. I'm Sean.'

'Nick.'

'You've been asking about Sandra Docherty, Nick?'

'Yes.'

'What've you got?'

'She gave evidence at an inquest in February 1975. She was one of five witnesses. Three are now dead.'

'Make that four.'

'What?'

'Four are dead.'

'What happened?'

'You're asking about Queensland's most notorious unsolved murder. I was a humble constable at the time. Sandra came to live in Brisbane in 1978. Her husband, Neil, was working in

Sydney during the week and coming home at weekends. It was supposed to be a temporary arrangement but it had gone on for a year or so. Anyway, he leaves on the Monday morning and then hears nothing further from her, which is unusual. So, he comes home early.'

'And he finds her decapitated?'

'Yes.'

'Body on the bed?'

'Yes.'

'Head in the sink?'

'In the bathroom, yes. How the fuck would you know that?'

'When was this?'

'July 3rd 1981.'

'Can you email me a copy of the post mortem report, Sean?'

'No problem. If you promise to keep me in the loop.'

'Gladly. Keep it under your hat for the time being, though. We haven't made an arrest yet.'

'Can you tell me any more? What's the story?'

'All of the victims were medics involved in the treatment of a two year old girl. She died of meningitis in 1974. The doctor was murdered in 1979 and Sandra Gibson in 1981. We've now got two more victims, killed within the last two weeks. I'm fairly sure they were killed by the child's father.'

'Revenge?'

'Looks like it.'

'Good luck, Nick. Email's on its way. Keep me posted, mate.'

'Will do.'

Dixon turned around. Everyone had been listening to his call.

'I suppose you all got that?'

'Yes, Sir,' replied Dave Harding.

'She was killed in an identical way to John Hawkins?' asked Mark Pearce.

'She was, Mark, yes,' replied Dixon. He turned to Dave Harding. 'What news of the paediatrician, Dave?'

'None, I'm afraid, Sir. Seems to have dropped off the radar.'

'Keep at it. If he's alive, we have to find him.'

'Yes, Sir.'

'Mark, now that we know what happened to Sandra Docherty, I want you to help Jane find the husband, David Southall. You help them too, Louise. I want to be kicking his bloody door down at 5 a.m. tomorrow morning, so get me an address.'

'Yes, Sir.'

'Well, I can account for Frances Southall,' continued Dixon.

'She's dead,' said Jane.

'21st October 1975. They were staying at the Hotel Senator in Marbella. She tied a rope to the radiator, put the other end around her neck and then jumped off the balcony.'

'Suicide by hanging.'

'That's only part of the story, Louise. The technical term is "external decapitation".'

'What does that mean?'

'The rope was too long for the weight of her body.' Dixon paused. 'The force of it pulling tight took her head clean off.'

'She was decapitated?'

'Explains a lot, doesn't it?'

Dixon parked across the drive of Dr Maunder's house on the out-skirts of Wedmore. It was a large property opposite the primary school on the main road into the village. There was a high stone wall fronting the road with evergreen shrubs planted along it. Dixon recognised camellias, azaleas and rhododendrons. The house was large, rendered and painted white. There were pink roses planted in tubs either side of the porch and a wisteria in a small flowerbed adjacent to the garage. It grew up the corner, then across the front of the house and over the porch. There was a brand new blue Volvo V70 parked in the drive.

Dixon knocked on the door. A large dog started barking. He could hear a woman's voice shouting.

'There's someone at the door, Eric.'

'You get it.'

A woman in her late sixties answered the door. She wore a brown denim skirt and black polo neck sweater. The fingers of her left hand were hooked in the collar of a large Dobermann pinscher.

'Yes?'

'I'm looking for Dr Maunder.'

'Are you selling something?'

'No. I'm a police officer.'

Dixon held up his warrant card.

'Wait here.' The woman closed the door. Dixon waited. A few moments later, the door reopened.

"You'd better come in.'

'And you are?' asked Dixon.

'Mrs Maunder.'

Dixon followed her up the stairs.

'He's in his office. He's writing a book.'

'What about?'

'Delville Wood.'

'Really?'

'You've heard of it?'

'Yes.'

Mrs Maunder pushed open a door off the first floor landing.

'The policeman's here, Eric. He can't be all bad. He's heard of Delville Wood.'

Dr Maunder looked up from his computer.

'You've heard of Delville Wood?'

'I went there a couple of years ago. I was on the Somme following my great grandfather's footsteps.'

Eric Maunder stood up from his desk and shook Dixon's hand. He was a tall man with thinning hair. He wore black jeans and a brown cable sweater.

'Which regiment was he in?'

'The Somerset Light Infantry. Second battalion.'

'They weren't at Delville Wood, surely?' asked Maunder.

'No. The sixth battalion were, I think, but not the second. But don't get me started on that. We'll be here all day and I'm afraid time is short.'

'Yes, sorry. How can I help?'

'Does the name Dr Ralph Vodden mean anything to you?'

'He was a doctor at Arundel House in the seventies. Left under a bit of a cloud, if I remember rightly.'

'Tell me about this cloud.'

'Now you're testing my memory. I remember that a child died. A baby girl.'

'Anything else?'

'The mother committed suicide a year or so later. It hit Vodden really hard.'

'Can you recall what happened to the father?'

'He was detained under the Mental Health Act. Sectioned or whatever it was in those days. It was after his wife killed herself. He went off the rails . . .' Maunder's voice tailed off.

'What?'

'It's coming back to me now. She hanged herself and was decapitated in the process. They were at a hotel in Spain or somewhere. He was by the pool and saw her jump.'

'How long was he detained for?'

'I don't know, I'm afraid.'

'What about Vodden?'

'It was the last straw for him. He left. Went to Norfolk, I think it was.'

'Is there anything else you can remember?'

'No. I'm sorry. It was a long time ago and I've been retired over ten years now too.'

'Well, thank you. You've been most helpful. Here's my card if you think of anything else.'

'Yes, of course. I'll give you a ring.'

'And good luck with the book.'

⌣

It was just before 4 p.m. when Dixon left Dr Maunder's house in Wedmore. He drove out of the village towards Burnham-on-Sea. It was drizzling with rain and getting dark, so he put his head-lights on.

He was deep in thought. He now had a clear picture in his mind of what had happened all those years ago. He was also able to answer the two crucial questions that had been bothering him: Why decapitation, and why the delay between Rosie's death in 1974 and the murder of Dr Vodden in 1979? He was convinced that Rosie's father, David Southall, murdered Vodden and then travelled to Australia to kill Sandra Gibson. He now needed evidence of it.

It would also be interesting to know what had happened to the paediatrician, Julian Spalding, if anything. But one substantive question remained: Why the delay of over thirty years until the murders of Valerie Manning and John Hawkins? He knew that he wouldn't find the answer to that question until he found David Southall. He reached for his phone and rang Jane.

'Jane, it's Nick. Any news of Southall?'

'Not yet. Where are you?'

'On my way back from Wedmore. Southall was sectioned after the death of his wife, which explains the delay before the murder of Dr Vodden in 1979. We need Southall's medical records.'

'I'll see what I can do. Are you all right?'

'Yes, why?'

'Your speech sounds a bit slurred. Have you been drinking?'

'Of course not. You sound like my mother.'

Dixon rang off and threw his phone onto the passenger seat. He tried to think of reasons for the thirty year gap between the murders. He had always considered it possible that it was a different killer, of course. That was too obvious a possibility to be overlooked.

Suddenly, the vision of Valerie Manning in the car park flashed across his mind. The knife glinted in the streetlights. Then he saw her on the slab in the mortuary. Frances Southall was standing next to him with Rosie in her arms.

Dixon blinked and shook his head. He felt light headed. He took his hand off the steering wheel and held it out in front of him. It was shaking. He had been diabetic long enough to know the signs. Jane had been right. His speech was usually the first to go.

He reached into his jacket pocket for his fruit pastilles. Coated in sugar, they always did the trick. He produced a handful of empty wrapping paper.

'Fuck it.'

He began to panic. He was sweating and could feel his legs beginning to weaken. It was becoming an effort to keep his foot on the accelerator and took all his concentration to keep driving. If he could make it to the village shop in Mark, he'd be fine.

He reached the outskirts of the village. He was driving slowly. Trying to hold the Land Rover in a straight line but, at the same time, he was desperate to reach the shop before he passed out.

'Fucking idiot.'

He remembered that there was usually a spare packet of sweets in the glove compartment. He reached across and fumbled with the catch. Suddenly, there was a loud bang. He looked up. He had a hit a parked car. It was red and small but that's all he knew. There was broken glass on the bonnet of his car. He kept driving.

He made it to the shop in Mark and parked with his front wheels on the village green and his rear wheels on the pavement. He switched the engine off but had no strength left to cross the road to the shop. He slumped over the steering wheel.

His phone rang. He reached across to the passenger seat but it was gone. He could see it on the floor in the footwell. He lay across the seat and picked it up.

'We've got a name.'

Dixon could not reply.

'Nick, it's Jane. Are you all right?'

'Sugar.'

'Where are you?'

'Mark. By the shop.'

'In your car?'

'Yes.'

'Can you make it to the shop?'

'No.'

Jane rang off. She picked up her handbag and ran out of the CID Room. She rang directory enquiries. She asked for Mark General Stores and was connected straight away.

'Can you help me? This is an emergency.'

'Yes.'

'Look out of the front window of your shop. Can you see a Land Rover?'

'Yes. It's parked half on the village green.'

'And the driver?'

'Slumped over the steering wheel.'

'He's having a diabetic episode. Can you take him a Lucozade drink and a Mars bar, please? This is really urgent. I'm on my way and will pay for it when I get there.'

'Yes, of course.'

Jane arrived twenty minutes later to find Dixon sitting on a bench opposite the shop. Monty was on his lead and sitting at Dixon's feet.

'Are you OK?'

'Getting there. Splitting headache.'

'What happened?'

'No lunch.'

'Idiot.'

Jane went into the shop and reappeared a few minutes later.

'They're very nice in there. Very helpful.'

'They are.'

'Give me your keys.'

Jane got into the Land Rover and reversed it off the village green. She then handed the keys back to Dixon.

'If anyone finds out about this I could lose my job,' he said.

'It's hardly the end of the world.'

'A hypo behind the wheel is a big deal for a diabetic. I could lose my licence. And I hit a parked car.'

'Where?'

'Back there, I think. It was red.'

Jane walked along the road in the direction of Wedmore. She came to a red Vauxhall Corsa with a dent in the driver's side front wing. The wing mirror was in pieces in the road. She walked back.

'Did you give them your name in the shop?'

'No.'

'Neither did I. Can you drive?'

'I should be OK now.'

'Get in and let's get the hell out of here.'

'What about . . . ?'

'They'll think it was farm machinery or something. The car's an old heap, anyway.'

———

Dixon followed Jane. They had reached Edithmead when Jane indicated left and pulled into a farm gateway. Dixon parked behind her. She got out and ran back. Dixon wound his window down. It had stopped raining.

'We've got an address. Louise just rang.'

'Where?'

'17 Mark Close, Highbridge.'

'Let's go and have a look. Pull into the Bristol Bridge Inn. We can leave your car there.'

'What are you going to do?

'Just a drive by. Don't panic. And what's his name? You never told me.'

'David John Selby. He got married in 1983 and took his wife's name rather than the other way round.'

Jane parked in the Bristol Bridge Inn car park and they continued in Dixon's Land Rover.

'It's off Maple Drive.'

Dixon turned into Maple Drive and then left into Mark Close. It was a short and narrow residential road with twelve bungalows on either side. All were constructed of red brick and appeared identical. Each had a bay window either side of the front door, a drive leading to a garage at the side, and a small area of lawn to the front, split by a garden path.

There was a turning circle at the far end of the Close. Dixon drove to the end and turned the Land Rover. He then drove slowly back along Mark Close, counting off the house numbers. Odd numbers were to his nearside.

Number 17 had a 'For Sale' board outside. There was a 'Sale Agreed' sticker across it. He stopped across the drive.

'It's empty,' said Jane.

'Go and have a look through the window.'

Jane ran up the drive. She looked in the first window then crossed the garden path and looked in the window on the other side. She ran back across the lawn.

'Empty.'

Dixon looked at the estate agent's sign.

'Let's pay them a visit.'

They arrived outside the estate agent's office in College Road, Burnham-on-Sea, just as it was closing. The door was locked but their warrant cards and some persistent knocking were sufficient to persuade him to unlock the door. The agent, Simon Perry, was happy to help in any way he could, once the importance and urgency had been explained to him.

He confirmed that Mr and Mrs David Selby were the owners of the property and that it was, indeed, sale agreed. The conveyancing was being handled by Humberstones Solicitors, whose offices were a few doors along College Road. The property had been cleared of its contents and Mrs Selby had moved in with her son, Richard, in Puriton. This was supposed to be a temporary arrangement. Mr Selby had moved into the Allandale Lodge Residential Care Home on Berrow Road.

There were some complications with the conveyancing transaction, which was on hold while Mr Selby's Lasting Power of Attorney was registered with the Office of the Public Guardian. The agent was confident that the buyer would wait.

Dixon asked for and was given copies of the Selbys' identity documents. Passports, driving licences and a copy of their gas and electricity bills. Dixon thanked Simon Perry very much for his help and reminded him that it was vital no one was informed that the police had been making enquiries.

Dixon and Jane sat in the Land Rover, listening to the rain hammering on the roof. Dixon was deep in thought.

'What does it mean that his Lasting Power of Attorney is being registered?' asked Jane.

'He's lost his fucking marbles, hasn't he?'

'What do we do, then?'

'We arrest him anyway. Two psychiatrists will decide whether he's fit to be interviewed. In the meantime, we get his medical records and speak to his wife. We can also get statements from the care home and the solicitor.'

'You know what this means?' asked Jane.

'If he really is mentally incapable and in a care home, then he can't have killed Valerie Manning or John Hawkins, can he?'

'Exactly.'

'Ring Dave and find out where he has got to with Spalding. We have to assume he is still in danger. Tell him to get everyone together for a briefing at 8 a.m. too.'

'What are we going to do?'

'Get your car. Fancy a bite to eat?'

'But . . .'

'He's not going anywhere, is he?'

Chapter Eight

Allandale Lodge Residential Care Home for the Elderly was a new, purpose built home on the corner of Rectory Road and Berrow Road, Burnham-on-Sea. A Google search told Dixon that it was home to thirty-one residents—thirty-two including David Southall. Dixon arrived with Jane just before 10 a.m. and rang the doorbell promptly on the hour. At precisely the same time, Dave Harding and Louise Willmott knocked on the door of David Southall's son, Richard, in Puriton.

Dixon was let in by a care assistant. He asked for the manager and was shown through to a small office adjacent to the kitchen. He glanced into the kitchen as he walked past and could see two carers, a man and a woman. They both wore light blue uniforms and were standing by the sink, drinking coffee. Dixon could hear the dishwasher running.

'Susan, two people to see you.'

The manager looked up from her computer.

'Can I help you?'

Dixon stepped to one side to allow Jane into the office and then closed the door behind them. Dixon showed her his warrant card.

'My name is Detective Inspector Nick Dixon. This is Detective Constable Jane Winter. And you are?'

'Sorry. Susan Procter.'

'Tell me about David Southall, or Selby, I suppose we have to call him now.'

'I really ought to ring his wife.'

'There's no need. She's on her way here now.'

'Well, he has vascular dementia. It's aggressive and early onset.'

'And from a practical point of view, that means what?'

'He's incapable. He doesn't even know who his wife is now.'

'Children?'

'Two sons. They visit from time to time. He doesn't know them either.'

'How long has he been here?'

'About four months, perhaps a bit longer.'

'And he's been incapable throughout that time?'

'Completely. It's amazing Mrs Selby was able to keep him at home as long as she did.'

'Is there any chance he could have left Allandale Lodge and returned unnoticed?'

'Definitely not. Not only is he incapable of it but the front door is locked at all times. That's to keep people in, not out.'

'Which room is he in?'

'Seven. In the ground floor annexe.'

'Can you show us, please?'

'Yes. Can I ask what for?'

'I'm going to arrest him for murder.'

'Oh, my God.'

'Can he be moved?'

'He's physically fit, so I suppose he could be, yes.'

'Who is his doctor?'

'He's still with his own GP in Highbridge at the moment. His records are going to be transferred to our doctor's surgery, though.'

'Which is?'

'Arundel House.'

Dixon looked at Jane. She shook her head.

'And the surgery in Highbridge?'

'Corner Place.'

Dixon turned back to Jane.

'Ring Mark, Jane, and get him over there now.'

Jane stepped outside the office to make the call.

'If I explain to Mr Selby that I am a police officer, will he understand what that means?' asked Dixon.

'No,' replied Susan Procter. 'He's gone, I'm afraid. He's beyond that.'

'Well, I need to make the arrest and then it'll be for two psychiatrists to decide whether he's fit to be interviewed.'

'Follow me.'

Dixon and Jane followed Susan Procter through the lounge to the ground floor annexe and along the corridor to David Selby's room. The door was propped open and a care assistant was clearing away a breakfast tray. David Selby was dressed. He wore brown corduroys, a blue check shirt, open at the neck, and a cardigan. He was sitting in an armchair facing the door. He was slumped forward, his eyes vacant and his mouth open. Dixon noticed that he was dribbling onto the collar of his shirt.

'Give us a minute, will you, Nikki?' said Susan Procter.

The care assistant wiped Selby's mouth with a tissue, picked up the tray and then left the room. Susan Procter closed the door behind her. The room contained a single hospital bed, a bedside table, pine wardrobe and matching chest of drawers. The only other item of furniture was the armchair that Selby was sitting in. Dixon noticed family photographs on the bedside table and on top of the chest of drawers.

Dixon reached into his jacket pocket and took out the photocopy of David Selby's passport. He passed it to Jane, who looked at it, nodded and then handed it back. Selby was older and he had lost weight, but it was definitely him. His face was thin, almost gaunt, and his eyes were deep set. His head was tipped to one side. He began dribbling onto his shirt collar again.

Dixon stepped forward and sat on the end of the bed opposite Selby.

'Mr Selby?'

There was no answer.

Susan Procter stood next to Selby, put her left arm around his shoulder and spoke directly into his right ear.

'David, there's a police officer to see you.'

Again, no response.

'I'm going to arrest him anyway, Mrs Procter. There'll then be a uniformed officer on the door to this room, with your permission, until the psychiatrists have been to assess him. If needs be, he can then be moved to a secure unit.'

'You do what you have to do, Inspector.'

Dixon turned to Selby.

'David John Selby, I am arresting you on suspicion of the murders of Ralph Ernest Vodden and Sandra Gwynneth Docherty. You do not have to say anything, but it may harm your defence if you do not mention when questioned something that you later rely on in court. Anything you do say may be given in evidence.'

'He's going to get away with it,' said Jane.

'I almost think he's been through enough already, don't you? And he's in a prison of sorts now anyway,' said Dixon.

'What will happen?' asked Susan Procter.

'The CPS will have to decide whether it's in the public interest to prosecute him. And I think we can all guess what the answer to that one will be,' replied Dixon.

Dixon was briefing the uniformed officers who would be keeping guard on David Selby for the time being, when Dave Harding and Louise Willmott arrived with Mrs Selby.

'She's not a happy bunny,' said Harding.

Mrs Selby was in her late sixties, with short dark hair, which was grey at the roots. A pair of glasses hung around her neck on a cord. She wore navy blue trousers and a black polo neck sweater under a dark green Barbour style jacket. She shouted across the roof of the car to Dixon.

'Are you in charge?'

'I am.'

'What the bloody hell is going on?'

'Come this way, Mrs Selby. We'll find a private room where we can have a chat.' Dixon turned to walk back into Allandale Lodge. He glanced across at Jane. 'You too, Jane.'

Susan Procter vacated her office. Dixon and Mrs Selby sat either side of the desk. Jane stood by the door.

'Mrs Selby, I'm sorry to have to tell you that I have just arrested your husband on suspicion of two counts of murder.'

'That's ridiculous. He's not capable . . .'

'How long have you known him?'

'We met in 1982 and married in 1983.'

'What did he tell you of his life before that?'

'Everything.'

'Then you know why we are here.'

Mrs Selby took a deep breath. She closed her eyes. When she opened them again they were full of tears. She did not reply.

'Don't you?'

'Yes.'

'I think that we need to continue this conversation down at the station, if you wouldn't mind accompanying us, Mrs Selby?'

Again, she did not reply.

Once outside, Dixon turned to Jane.

'Take a panda car, Jane. Sit her in an interview room and let her sweat.'

'Where are you going?'

'To look at some family photographs. I'll catch you up.'

Dixon paused in the hall and looked at himself in the mirror on the wall above the visitors' book. He was wearing light trousers, a blue and white striped shirt, red tie and navy blazer. He was clean shaven and looked smart enough. But he did not like what he saw.

He was at risk of losing his driving licence and his job. Pure stupidity and he knew it. Leaving aside the hypo behind the wheel that would cost him his licence, he had failed to stop at the scene of an accident and failed to report it. Traffic offences they may be, but they implied an element of dishonesty that would not go down well at a disciplinary hearing. It was out of his hands, of course. It would all depend on the owner of the Vauxhall Corsa reporting the damage to the police. Dixon would know soon enough. A diabetic in a Land Rover and the owner of Mark Stores would be able to give a description of the driver. Even PC Cole would be able to solve that one.

And what about Jane? She now had something on him. He would need to make sure he didn't fall out with her, although she would be slitting her own throat if she reported him. Dixon winced. It was an unfortunate choice of words.

He straightened his tie and walked through the lounge towards David Selby's room. No good worrying about it now.

David Selby was asleep in his armchair. His head was tipped to one side and his mouth was open. The radio was on, playing loud pop music. Dixon switched it off. He looked around the room. There were several framed photographs on the bedside table and more on the chest of drawers. He looked at each in turn.

On the bedside table was a colour photograph of Selby and his wife on their wedding day. She was wearing a pink dress and Dixon recognised the Burnham Registry Office. There was also a picture of Selby standing on the beach holding a Jack Russell and one of him on a boat with two boys, presumably his two sons from his second marriage. The photographs on the chest of drawers were much the same, but included several of elderly relatives, who Dixon assumed to be Selby's parents, and others of him and Mrs Selby on various holidays. Dixon thought he recognised the Lake District. The rest appeared to have been taken in Greece or perhaps on some Greek Island.

Dixon had learned nothing new. He looked around the room. David Selby was still asleep. There were no books or magazines anywhere, but then reading was well beyond Selby now. Dixon looked in the wardrobe and also the chest of drawers. As expected, he found nothing of interest amongst the clothes.

The top drawer of the bedside table contained several pairs of spectacles, packets of sweets and not much else. Dixon opened the small cupboard underneath and found two half eaten boxes of chocolates, an empty address book and a small photograph album.

He sat on the edge of the bed to look through it. It reminded him of the album that his mother had put together for his grandmother. He had spent many an hour going through it with her, triggering memories with each picture. Clearly, someone had done the same for Selby.

Each photograph was annotated in pencil. 'David aged 1' through to the inevitable school uniform shot, 'David first day at King Alfred's'. There were photos of Selby with his parents, in various football teams and then the last of the black and white photographs taken at his graduation from Durham University.

The photographs then switched to colour and began with more wedding shots, 'David and Jean Wedding 30th September 1983'. The gap was obvious. Not a single photograph of his first wife, Frances, or his daughter, Rosie. Maybe none existed, or perhaps Mrs Selby did not want to trigger bad memories. Dixon made a mental note to ask her. He also noticed that there were no photographs of their two sons as infants. Another question for Mrs Selby. He flicked through the remaining photographs in the album. None were particularly interesting. Selby appeared to enjoy sea fishing from a boat and latterly with his two sons, but that was the only conclusion Dixon was able to reach.

The photographs ended several pages before the back of the album, leaving the last few pages blank. Dixon continued to turn the pages, although he was no longer looking at them. David Selby was stirring. He opened his eyes and looked at Dixon. Selby yawned, closed his eyes and then was gone again. Dixon looked down. Inside the back cover of the album was a loose photograph. It was black and white, curled at the corners and, judging by the line down the middle, had once been folded in half. Dixon picked it up, unfolded the corners and looked at it intently. He recognised a young David Selby. Older than at his graduation but younger than on his wedding to Jean Selby. He was sitting in a deck chair on a beach. Next to him, also in a deck chair, sat a young woman. Dixon knew he was looking at Frances Southall. In front of her on the sand sat a young child wearing a nappy. She was holding a small spade and appeared to be hitting an upturned bucket with it. That must be Rosie, thought Dixon. Behind her stood a small boy in swimming trunks. Three or perhaps four years old. He was looking down at the girl and smiling. Dixon recognised the smile of an older brother. He looked at Selby and then back to the photograph. He turned it over. There was a pencil note on the back, 'Dawlish Warren June 1974'. He noticed that David Selby was looking at him.

'You had a son, David?'

Dixon felt sure that he saw a flicker of recognition in Selby's eyes. Then he was gone again.

Dixon put the photograph in his inside jacket pocket. Then he closed the album, replaced it in the bedside cabinet and left David Selby asleep.

———

Dixon arrived at Burnham-on-Sea Police Station just after 11.30 a.m. Jane was waiting for him in the reception area.

'She's asked for a solicitor. Poole's on his way from Ashtons in Weston. He'll be here in about twenty minutes.'

'Is everyone here?'

'Except Dave. He's organising the reconstruction for later today.'

'Has he found Spalding?'

'Not yet.'

'What about Selby's medical records?'

'Mark has got them.'

Dixon walked into the CID Room. Mark Pearce was reading Selby's medical records. Louise Willmott was on her computer.

'Let me have those, Mark.'

'Yes, Sir,' replied Pearce, bundling up the records.

'Right then, Louise and I will interview Mrs Selby.'

'But . . .'

'Jane, I want you and Mark to find the son.'

'Which one? He's got two.'

'Wrong. He's got three.'

'Three?' asked Jane.

'Yes. He had a son by his first wife.'

'Rosie had a brother?' asked Louise.

'She did.'

'What was his name?'

'I don't know yet. Mrs Selby will know.'

'He wasn't on Vodden's patient lists,' said Jane.

'He wasn't, which is odd. Maybe he was a patient of another doctor in the same surgery? But top priority is to find him.'

'Do we know what happened to him?'

'He was probably taken into care, unless he went to live with relatives. He was only three or four at the time, remember. Start with Social Services.'

'It's Saturday, don't forget,' said Jane.

'Ring the emergency line. Then kick their door down if you have to,' replied Dixon. 'And we need to pick up his other two sons as well. Richard is in Puriton and Marcus in London, so get onto the Met.'

Dixon sat at a vacant desk and opened Selby's medical records. The cover had been amended to reflect his change of name. Southall had been crossed out and Selby written above it. Dixon leafed through the letters and medical reports attached. He found a report, a little over a year old, from a consultant psychiatrist in elderly client medicine confirming the diagnosis of vascular dementia. A further report from an occupational therapist dated 11th May recommended an urgent move into residential care on the grounds that Mrs Selby was no longer able to cope with him at home. Selby was described as suffering from advanced vascular dementia. He had suffered a 'significant episode' over Easter, which had resulted in a dramatic deterioration in his condition. His Addenbrooke's Cognitive Examination score was unusually low and he was far from mentally capable. The OT also recommended registration of his lasting power of attorney.

Dixon looked through the older documents. He found a letter from Dr Vodden dated 17th January 1976. It was a referral to a consultant psychiatrist recommending that David Southall be sectioned under the Mental Health Act. Southall had been unable to deal with the loss of his daughter and then the suicide of his wife. He was a risk to himself and his son, Martin, and he had, according to Dr Vodden, 'stuck his head in the sand'.

Dixon handed the letter to Jane.

'Read this.'

He watched Jane reading the letter, waiting for her to reach the relevant passage.

'Oh, for fuck's sake.'

'Precisely,' said Dixon.

'What a shitty thing to say about a man who'd lost his wife and child,' said Jane.

'It is. But at least we now know why Vodden's head was left in a bunker. And we've got a name for the son.'

The interview with Jean Selby began at 2 p.m in an interview suite at Burnham-on-Sea Police Station. Dixon had deliberately kept her waiting, despite protests from her solicitor, Mr Poole.

'I really must protest, Inspector. My client is not under arrest and to keep her waiting nearly three hours is unacceptable.'

'I can arrest her, if you prefer, Mr Poole.'

'What for?'

'Perverting the course of justice, assisting an offender, take your pick.'

Jean Selby glared at Poole.

'Now, shall we make a start?' asked Dixon.

Jean Selby nodded.

Dixon made the introductions for the tape. He reminded Mrs Selby that she was not under arrest and was free to leave at any time.

'When did you meet David Southall?'

'We met in 1982 and married the following year. I told you that.'

'You did. You also said that he told you everything about his life before you met. What exactly did he tell you?'

'That his daughter had been killed by incompetent doctors and first wife had committed suicide soon after.'

'What else?'

'He went to pieces and ended up being sectioned.'

'And when he was released?'

Jean Selby looked at Poole and then back to Dixon. She was twisting her wedding band around her ring finger with her right index finger and thumb. She took a deep breath and exhaled slowly.

'He went after them.'

'Who?'

'The doctors. The people he blamed . . . held responsible.'

'And what did he do to them?'

'He killed the doctor and his receptionist.'

'How?'

'You already know the answers to these questions.'

'We need to hear it from you.'

'His wife was decapitated when she hanged herself. So he stabbed them . . . and then decapitated them.'

'Let's start with the doctor, then. What was his name?'

'Dr Vodden.'

'What happened?'

'It's on the Internet, Inspector. Read it for yourself.'

'I need to know what you know, Mrs Selby.'

'Not a lot. He didn't go into graphic detail. Just that he killed him, cut his head off, dumped the body and set fire to the car.'

'Is that it?'

'The doctor said that David had stuck his head in the sand, so he did the same to him.'

'What about the receptionist?'

'He flew to Australia to kill her. Brisbane, I think it was. Again, it's on the Internet.'

'And you knew this when you married him?'

'Yes.'

Dixon looked at Louise Willmott.

'I loved him, Inspector,' said Jean Selby. 'You need to understand, he was mentally ill at the time he did it. He was a different person when I met him.'

'You were qualified to make that assessment?'

'I was, actually. I was his community psychiatric nurse. That's how we met.'

'And you never thought to tell the police that he had murdered two people in cold blood?'

'I knew I should, but I couldn't do it. I loved him.'

'So, why are you telling us now?'

'Look at him. What can you possibly do to him now?'

Tears were streaming down Jean Selby's cheeks.

'What about his innocent victims and their families?'

'They weren't innocent!' snapped Jean Selby. 'They killed his wife and child. And look what the stress of it has done to him . . .' Her voice tailed off and she began to sob.

'I think this has gone on long enough, Inspector,' said Poole. 'So, unless you have any further questions . . . ?'

'I do, as it happens. Several,' replied Dixon. 'Tell me about your sons. It's Richard and Marcus, isn't it?'

'What've they got to do with it?'

'Let me be quite clear, Mrs Selby. I am investigating the murders of Dr Ralph Vodden in 1979 and also that of his receptionist, Sandra Docherty, in 1981. You have just told me that your husband, David John Southall, otherwise known as David John Selby, committed those murders.'

'Yes.' Jean Selby had stopped crying and was listening intently to Dixon.

'I am also investigating the murders of Valerie Manning and John Hawkins. Both were killed within the last two weeks. They were stabbed and then decapitated. What can you tell me about their deaths?'

'Nothing.'

'Both were involved in the treatment of Rosie Southall and gave evidence at her inquest.'

Jean Selby looked at Poole. She said nothing.

'The general consensus seems to be that your husband is not capable of that.'

'Of course not.'

'So, who did it?'

'I don't know.'

'So, we come back to your sons . . .'

'They've got nothing to do with it.' Jean Selby started shaking. 'They know nothing about it.'

'About what?'

'His past.'

'We'll need to interview them and take DNA.'

'You can't do that!' screamed Mrs Selby. She turned to Mr Poole. 'They can't do that. Stop them.'

'Is this really necessary, Inspector?' said Poole.

'Yes.'

'You can't . . .'

'Mrs Selby, perhaps it would be better if you told me why we can't.'

She began to sob again. She covered her face with her hands. Dixon waited for her to regain her composure.

'They're adopted. The DNA won't match.' She spoke in between sobs and was struggling to catch her breath. 'They don't know. We never told them. It'll break their hearts.'

'And what about your stepson?'

The effect was immediate. Jean Selby stopped crying and stared at Dixon. He reached into his pocket and produced the crumpled black and white photograph. He placed it on the table in front of her. Mrs Selby picked it up and looked at it before placing it back on the table.

'It was in the photograph album, Mrs Selby.'

Dixon waited.

'Martin. He was adopted in 1976. Marcus and Richard don't know about him.'

'Has he ever made contact with his father?'

'No.'

'Where is he?'

'I really don't know.'

'What was his adoptive name?'

'I don't know.'

'Did your husband ever try to find him?'

'No.'

'Did he talk about him or wonder what became of him, perhaps?'

'No. It was a part of his life he tried to forget.'

'His own son?'

'Unless you have been in that situation, Inspector, you will never understand.'

'I've heard enough,' said Dixon. 'This interview is terminated at 2.27 p.m.' He got up to leave the room.

'I'm assuming my client is free to leave, Inspector,' said Poole.

'Mr Poole, if your client attempts to leave the station, she will be arrested on suspicion of perverting the course of justice.'

⸺

Dixon and Louise Willmott went back up to the CID room. It was empty, apart from Dave Harding, who was eating a sandwich.

'Where is everybody?' asked Dixon.

'Jane and Mark have gone to meet someone from Social Services at County Hall. They left about twenty minutes ago.'

'What about Richard and Marcus Selby?'

'Richard is on his way here and the Met have picked up Marcus. They are checking alibis and a DNA sample will be couriered down here overnight.'

'Any news on Spalding?'

'No, Sir. I'm waiting to hear from the DWP but it's the weekend, of course. The reconstruction is set for 5 p.m. onwards, though.'

'Good.'

Dixon turned to Louise Willmott.

'Let's keep Mrs Selby in tonight, Louise, while we speak to her precious sons and track down Martin Southall. Arrest her for perverting the course of justice and stick her in a cell. We can release her on police bail tomorrow but don't tell her that.'

'Yes, Sir.'

Dixon looked at his watch.

'Do me a favour, will you, Dave? Check with SOCO to see if they got any DNA off that wine glass at John Hawkins' place.'

'Yes, Sir.'

'I'm just nipping out for a bite to eat.'

Chapter Nine

Dixon drove around to the seafront. He parked in the Morrisons car park close to the spot where Valerie Manning had parked, bought a small bag of chips from the takeaway in Abingdon Street and then sat on the sea wall next to the jetty to eat them. He threw Monty's tennis ball along the beach and watched as he tore off after it.

All he could do was wait. Martin Southall was the obvious priority, but Dixon knew that without a name for his adoptive parents, it was going to be difficult to make any real progress. He needed to be found before he got to Spalding, the consultant paediatrician and the last of Rosie Southall's inquest witnesses still alive.

Dixon found it difficult not to have some sympathy for Martin Southall. He had watched his little sister die in his mother's arms and then had had to endure his mother's suicide. As if that wasn't enough, his father had then suffered a mental breakdown. He had lost his entire family by the time he was five years old. Shit happens, thought Dixon, but Martin Southall had someone to blame for his misfortune. Someone criticised for it in a court of law. And he was exacting his revenge. Finishing what his father had started. Martin Southall had to be found.

Dixon felt like a jockey whose horse refused to leave the stalls. The race was on but all he could do was watch it unfold. And throw the ball for his dog.

———⌣———

Dixon was back at Burnham Police Station by 4 p.m. There was still no news from Jane. Dave Harding was interviewing Richard Selby, who had arrived in a panda car escorted by two uniformed officers. Mrs Selby had been moved to a cell in the custody suite at Bridgwater Police Station, much to the annoyance of her solicitor, Mr Poole.

DCI Lewis and the Press Officer, Vicky Thomas, were waiting for Dixon in the CID Room.

'Where is everybody, Nick? What's going on?'

'We've found David Southall, Sir. He's suffering from vascular dementia and is in the Allandale Lodge Care Home. His wife has confirmed that he killed Dr Vodden and also Vodden's receptionist, Sandra Docherty. She had emigrated to Australia and was found decapitated in 1981.'

'What about Valerie Manning and the paramedic?'

'John Hawkins. No, he didn't kill them. He's incapable, to say the least. I've got two psychiatrists lined up to assess him on Monday.'

'So, who did?'

'We're looking for his son from his first marriage, Martin. He was five years old when his sister died.'

'You've got the wife in the cells too?'

'That's Southall's second wife, Sir. Jean Selby. His first wife, Frances, committed suicide after Rosie's death. She hanged herself and was decapitated in the process.'

'Decapitated?'

'Yes, Sir. Southall then suffered a breakdown and was sectioned.'

'Which explains the delay before the murder of Dr Vodden, I suppose?'

'It does.'

'So, what happened to the son?'

'We're trying to find out. Jane is at Social Services now.'

'Poor little bastard. His sister dies, his mother commits suicide and then his father goes nuts.'

'It's difficult not to feel sorry for him.'

'We don't really need this reconstruction, then?' asked Lewis.

'It's too late cancel it now,' said Vicky Thomas.

'Quite. We'll go ahead anyway. You never know what might come out of it.'

'We might as well, Sir,' said Dixon.

'Good work, though, Nick.'

'It will be if we can find the son before he gets to Spalding.'

'Remind me, who's Spalding?'

'The last of the witnesses who gave evidence at Rosie Southall's inquest. Dave's been on it but hasn't found him yet. He's not dead. We know that much.'

'Keep at it, then, and keep me posted too.'

'Yes, Sir.'

'Will you be at the reconstruction?'

'I'll be there, yes.'

'We'd best get over there now,' said Vicky Thomas, 'the press will be arriving soon.'

'Right. See you later, Nick,' said Lewis.

Dave Harding held the door open for DCI Lewis and Vicky Thomas to leave the room. Then he handed Richard Selby's statement to Dixon.

'Anything interesting?'

'Not really, Sir. Alibi seems perfectly reasonable to me, but I'll get uniform to check it out when they take him home. I've got a DNA swab.'

'Well done, Dave. You'd better head over to the reconstruction. I'll catch you up.'

'Yes, Sir.'

'Remind me where you got to with Spalding.'

'Waiting to hear from the DWP and NHS Pensions with bank details. His pensions are still being paid, but the address they have for him has other occupants, according to the electoral roll.'

'It could be let? Have you knocked on the door?'

'Not yet.'

Dixon frowned.

'I'll do it after the reconstruction, Sir.'

Dixon arrived at the Morrisons car park just before 5 p.m. All the roads were closed but he was allowed through the police cordon. He parked on the far side, well away from the reconstruction. It was dark, but the area was well lit by street lighting and the lights in the supermarket, which was still open. He could see a red Fiat Uno parked adjacent to the bus stop opposite the Pier Tavern and several film crews and photographers waiting nearby. A large crowd of onlookers was watching from outside the pub. He took out his phone and sent Jane a text message.

Any news?

He walked over to the bus stop to find Dave Harding briefing a group of uniformed officers under the supervision of Police Sergeant Dean. Each was given leaflets to hand out. He spotted DCI Lewis giving a television interview under the supermarket canopy. Vicky Thomas was standing close by, listening in.

Dixon watched as Dave Harding walked over to a police van parked on the other side of the road, outside Fortes ice cream parlour. Harding opened the back of the van and spoke to the occupants. A figure then stepped out of the back of the van. Dixon winced when he recognised PC Cole. He was wearing grey trainers, black trousers and a black or navy blue hooded top, Dixon couldn't tell in the artificial light. Cole was carrying a black holdall.

Dixon watched the reconstruction unfold from under the canopy of Morrisons. PC Cole did his best to loiter unobtrusively in and around the bus stop. He then walked over to the jetty and back several times, each stage being filmed for the evening news. He walked with his head down and covered by the hood of his top. A WPC played the part of Valerie Manning and together they created an accurate reconstruction of Valerie's abduction. Uniformed police officers mingled with the crowd handing out leaflets and asking questions. Dixon could see more of them in the Reeds Arms and Morrisons doing the same.

Dixon noticed two officers in animated conversation with possible witnesses, one with an elderly couple in the foyer of the supermarket, and the other outside the Pier Tavern. Dixon gestured to Dave Harding, who came over. Dixon pointed out the witnesses to Harding.

'Dave, it looks like we have someone who thinks they saw something. Find out what they've got to say, will you?'

Dave Harding walked over and spoke to each of the officers in turn, first the officer in Morrisons and then outside the Pier Tavern. He jogged back across the road to where Dixon was standing.

'The guy in the pub is a time waster. The elderly couple were doing their weekly shop and remember seeing someone carrying a black bag.'

'What time?'

'Same time. They always shop same time, same day every week.'

'Male or female?'

'They don't know.'

'What was this person wearing?'

'They can't remember.'

'Is there anything they can remember?'

'Just that the person was smaller than Cole.'

'Is that it?'

"Fraid so.'

Dixon looked at PC Cole. He was of medium height and medium build, possibly five feet ten or eleven inches and twelve stone. 'Smaller than Cole' described half the population. Dixon looked across the car park. The elderly couple were loading their shopping into the back of their car. He was about to walk over to question them further when his phone rang.

'We've got a name,' said Jane, as soon as Dixon answered.

'Well?'

'He spent time in two foster homes before he was adopted by a Mr and Mrs Cromwell. They lived in Yeovil at the time. I've got an address but it's going back to the late seventies.'

'Where are you now?'

'We're on our way back to the station.'

'I'll meet you there.'

Dixon rang off.

'Gotta go, Dave. Check that address for Spalding and keep me posted.'

'Yes, Sir.'

Dixon arrived at Burnham Police Station just after Jane and Mark Pearce. Jane was sitting at a computer. Pearce was standing behind her, looking at the screen.

'I've searched the PNC and they're not known to police. Nothing on the drivers' database, either,' said Jane.

'What about Martin Cromwell?'

'Nothing.'

'Try the electoral roll. What are their full names?' asked Dixon.

'Victoria Katherine Cromwell and Eric Cromwell.'

Dixon sat down in front of at a computer. He opened a web browser and went to Google. He typed 'Eric Cromwell announcement' into the search field and hit the 'Enter' button. All of the results on the first page came from iannounce.co.uk. He scrolled down and clicked on the third result, 'Eric Cromwell Death Notices, South-west England'.

'How about this?' Dixon read aloud. 'Eric Cromwell, on 7th November 2007 at Exmouth Community Hospital, aged 81. Formerly resident in Knowle Road, Yeovil. Beloved husband of Vicky and father to Martin. Funeral service at St Paul's Chapel, Exeter Crematorium on 22nd November at 3.15 p.m. Any enquiries via Caunters Funeral Service. Family flowers only.'

'How did you find that?' asked Jane.

'Google the name followed by 'announcement'. Try the wife.'

Dixon watched while Jane typed and then hit 'Enter'. He followed her eyes as she scanned the screen.

'Nothing.'

'Chances are she's still alive, then,' said Dixon. 'Get onto Exmouth police. We need an address and it would be good if they would kindly send a car to check it out. If she's in we need to know straight away.'

'Leave it with me.'

'Mark, check the electoral roll for Exmouth, will you?'

'Will do.'

Dixon poured himself a drink from the water tower.

'Nothing on the electoral roll, Sir.'

'That's not the end of the world. You can opt out these days. Try ringing the funeral directors, Caunters.'

'At this time on a Saturday?'

'They'll have a twenty-four hour emergency line. People don't always die between 9 a.m. and 5 p.m. Monday to Friday.'

'Yes, Sir.'

Both Jane and Mark Pearce were on the phone. Dixon tried to keep up with both conversations. Jane's finished first.

'They've got an address in Hulham Road, wherever that is. They're sending a car now.'

Mark Pearce's call ended.

'No luck with Caunters. They won't have access to their computer until Monday morning.'

'Thanks, Mark. You may as well head off. Be back here at 8 a.m. sharp.'

'Thank you, Sir.'

'What do we do now?' asked Jane.

'We wait. What number did you give them?'

'My mobile.'

'Good. Have you had lunch?'

'Lunch? No.'

'Let's go and get you something to eat, then.'

———

It was just before 7.30 p.m. when Jane's telephone rang. They were sitting in the bay window at the Dunstan House Hotel. Dixon was halfway through a gammon steak and chips. Jane was picking at the remains of her chicken curry. She fumbled in her handbag to find her phone.

'Jane Winter.'

Dixon listened to Jane's end of the conversation.

'Yes . . . thank you . . . did you try the neighb . . . when was this?'

Jane took a pen from the side pocket of her handbag and scribbled on a paper napkin.

'Yes . . . Princess Elizabeth Orthopaedic Centre . . . Royal Devon and Exeter Hosp . . . got it, thanks . . . which ward is she on? . . . Dyball . . . thank you.'

She turned the paper napkin around and slid it across the table to Dixon.

'One last thing. Have the neighbours seen her son recently? . . . Are you still sat outside the house? . . . Sorry to be a pain, but could you go and ask them, please? And then ring me straight back . . . thank you . . . yes . . . thanks.'

Jane rang off.

Dixon picked up the napkin. 'What the f . . . ?'

'It's not what you think. She's had a new hip. The neighbour dropped her at the hospital this morning. She had the operation this afternoon, apparently.'

'Is she all right?'

'He didn't know.'

Dixon took his iPhone out of his jacket pocket. He opened the web browser and navigated to Google. He typed in 'exeter hospital'. The Royal Devon and Exeter Hospital was the first result. He wrote down the telephone number on the corner of the napkin and then proceeded to dial it. When he had finished dialling, he got up and walked outside to make the call in the comparative privacy of the car park. It was dark, but the lights from the hotel lit up the car park. Dixon stood by the bay window.

'Dyball Ward, please.'

He waited for the click.

'Dyball Ward.'

'This is Detective Inspector Nick Dixon of Avon and Somerset Police. Can you tell me whether you have a Mrs Cromwell on the ward?'

'Well I . . .'

'Who am I speaking to?'

'Staff nurse Julie Pritchard.'

'Listen to me very carefully, Julie. I am who I say I am and this is a murder investigation. Now, do you . . . ?'

'Yes.'

'Is she in a fit state to answer questions?'

'No. She's not long out of recovery. She only had her op late afternoon so she's very groggy still.'

'When do you think . . . ?'

'It's unlikely to be until tomorrow, really. She'll be on morphine overnight.'

'Do you have her next of kin's contact details in her records?'

'Yes, it's her son, I think. I'll check. Hold on.'

Dixon's heart was racing. He could hear papers rustling.

'Yes, it's her son, Martin Cromwell. We've only got a mobile number, though . . .'

Dixon opened his mouth to speak but Julie continued.

'Do you want to speak to him now? He's sitting by her bed.'

Dixon banged on the window of the Dunstan House and waved at Jane to come outside.

'Where are you, Julie?'

'I'm out by the nurses' station. Is there a problem?'

'This is very important, Julie. I need you to act as if nothing has happened. Do you understand?'

'Yes.'

'Don't speak to anyone about this conversation and most of all, do not approach Martin Cromwell. Is that clear?'

'Yes. What's going on?'

'Just let him sit there as long as he wants. We'll be there as quick as we can.'

'Visiting time finishes at 8 p.m.'

Dixon looked at his watch. Twenty minutes.

'Don't ask him to leave, whatever you do, Julie. Let him sit there. We're on our way.'

'He's not a murderer, is he?' There was panic in Julie's voice.

'We just need to speak to him, that's all. Just go about your business in the usual way and forget he's there. OK?'

'Yes, OK.'

Dixon rang off just as Jane's phone rang. She answered it.

'Hello.'

'Three months . . . OK, thank you for that . . .'

Dixon interrupted. 'Is that Exmouth?'

'Yes.'

Dixon snatched Jane's phone from her hand.

'This is Detective Inspector Nick Dixon. Who am I speaking to?'

'PC Venables, Sir. Exmouth.'

'Right then, Constable Venables. We have a situation and I need your help.'

'Yes, Sir.'

'The suspect in a triple murder investigation, one Martin Cromwell, is currently sitting by his mother's bedside in Dyball Ward at the Royal Devon and Exeter Hospital. We are on our way now but it will take us at least an hour to get there. I need you to get on the radio and get any and every officer within a ten mile radius to converge on Dyball Ward now. Can you do that?'

'Leave it to me, Sir.'

'Visiting time finishes at 8 p.m. so he'll be leaving soon.'

'I understand.'

'We are leaving now and will get there as quick as we can. Please keep us abreast of developments on this number.'

'Will do, Sir.'

Dixon rang off and handed the phone back to Jane.

'He's at the hospital now?' asked Jane.

'He is.'

'Bloody hell.'

'Quite,' said Dixon. 'C'mon, we need to get going.'

'Have you settled up for the food?'

'I'll ring 'em from the car and tell them we'll pop back later. You drive.'

Dixon and Jane raced out of Burnham towards the M5. Jane managed to get Dixon's old Land Rover up to seventy-five miles per hour on the long straight before the railway bridge, but the noise made conversation difficult. Dixon was sitting in the passenger seat, shouting into his phone.

'We'll call in later to settle the bill . . . yes . . . police . . . yes . . . emergency . . . possibly tomorrow . . . sorry.'

He rang off.

'That's the Dunstan House sorted out. They're fine.'

'Good,' replied Jane.

She turned onto the M5 and headed south. It was a bright moonlit night. Dixon sat with his own phone in his right hand and Jane's in his left. He watched the traffic flashing past them in the outside lanes and began to wonder whether he had made such a wise choice of vehicle. Still, other officers were no doubt converging on Exeter hospital already and whatever vehicle they were in, Dixon and Jane could play no part in that. He looked at his watch. It would be at least 8.30 p.m. before they got there, assuming they didn't get lost. He could do nothing but wait. He looked at the stars in the night sky and watched the fireworks going off in Bridgwater from the bridge over the River Parrett.

'What's the time?' shouted Jane.

Dixon looked at his watch again. 'Gone eight.'

'They must be there by now.'

'They must.'

They drove on, listening to the roar of the Land Rover's old diesel engine. They had reached Taunton when Jane's phone lit up and then began ringing. Jane eased off the accelerator to reduce the engine noise. Dixon answered the call.

'DI Dixon.'

'This is Sergeant Hargreaves, Sir, Exeter Police. I'm afraid we missed him.'

Dixon gritted his teeth. He turned to Jane and shook his head.

'Fuck it,' muttered Jane, but it was lost in the engine noise.

'We've checked the bus stops but he's not there, either. He left about ten to eight, I'm told, Sir.'

'What time did you get there?' asked Dixon.

'The first car got here just after that. They missed him by a couple of minutes at most, according to the ward staff.'

'Is Nurse Pritchard there?'

'She's doing the changeover, Sir. The night shift are just coming on.'

'We're on our way, Sergeant, and will be there in about half an hour. Can you see to it that Nurse Pritchard stays? I'll need to speak to her.'

'Yes, Sir.'

'And the CCTV. We'll need a look at that.'

'I'll see what I can do, Sir.'

'Thank you, Sergeant. I'll ring you on this number when we get there.'

Dixon turned to Jane.

'They missed him. They bloody well missed him.'

'By how much?'

'A couple of minutes.'

'Typical.'

'Put your foot down and let's get there as quick as we can.'

The Royal Devon and Exeter Hospital was well signposted from Junction 30 on the M5 and it was just before 8.45 p.m. when Dixon and Jane turned off Barrack Road into the main entrance. They followed the signs for the Princess Elizabeth Orthopaedic Centre, which took them past the visitor car parks and into the hospital one way system. They were just beginning to think they might be lost when they recognised the Orthopaedic Centre on the left. It had two police cars parked outside and two more in the small car park opposite.

They parked in the car park next to one of the panda cars. Dixon reached into a cardboard box in the passenger footwell behind the driver's seat. He produced a blue light and placed it on the roof of the Land Rover.

'Cheaper than buying a parking ticket.'

The Princess Elizabeth Orthopaedic Centre was a three storey red brick and glass building attached to the main hospital. It had a large green canopy over the front doors and a small forecourt for use by ambulances and taxis. Dixon and Jane walked in to find the large reception area deserted.

'It is Saturday night, I suppose,' said Jane.

Dixon looked at a large map on the wall.

'Upstairs,' he said. He turned around, looking for either the stairs or the lift.

'Over here,' said Jane, walking towards large double doors on the far side of the foyer.

Once on the second floor, they followed the signs for Dyball Ward and arrived at the nurses' station to find three uniformed police officers in conversation with two nurses, one in light blue and the other dark blue. Dixon had never understood the colour coding of hospital uniforms. He presented his warrant card.

'I'm looking for Sergeant Hargreaves and Nurse Pritchard.'

'I'm Julie Pritchard,' said the nurse in the dark blue uniform. She was sitting back in an office chair holding a cup of tea in both hands.

'Sergeant Hargreaves has gone to the security office, Sir,' said one of the police officers.

'CCTV?'

'Yes, Sir.'

'Good,' said Dixon. He turned to Julie Pritchard. 'Is there somewhere we can have a word?'

'We can use the day room,' said Julie, getting up. 'It'll be empty now.'

Dixon and Jane followed her back along the corridor and into a room on the right. It contained a number of tables and chairs, two reclining chairs and a television, which was switched off. Dixon noticed the usual collection of two year old magazines and a jigsaw puzzle half done on one of the tables.

Julie Pritchard was tall and slim, with dark hair tied back into a ponytail. She wore dark blue trousers, a dark blue top and light blue crocs. She sat opposite Dixon at one of the tables. Jane sat to her left.

'I'm Nick Dixon. We spoke on the phone.'

'We did.'

'This is Detective Constable Jane Winter.'

Jane nodded.

'You went off duty at eight, I gather, Julie?' asked Dixon.

'Yes.'

'Thank you for staying behind.'

'It's fine. Is this anything to do with those murders on the news? The beheadings . . . ?'

'I really can't say, Julie,' replied Dixon.

'Of course you can't, sorry,' said Julie.

'Tell me about Mrs Cromwell.'

'There's not much to tell, to be honest. She only came up to the ward late so I've not had a chance to speak to her, really. She's had a new hip. She's on a morphine infusion pump at the moment and will be overnight, probably.'

'What about the son, Martin?'

'He'd been here all day, apparently. He waited with her until she went down and then hung around until she came out of recovery.'

'Did you speak to him?'

'Yes. Before you rang.'

'What did you say?'

'Just small talk, really. He asked if it was OK to sit with her and I said "fine". It was about 5.30 p.m. and visiting time hadn't started officially, you see?'

'What else?'

'I asked him if she was his mum and he said she was. Then I assured him she'd be all right and that was about it. He seemed really nice.'

'Describe him to me.'

Jane was making notes.

'He's late thirties, possibly forty or so. Tall.' Julie shrugged.

'Hair?' asked Dixon.

'Brown, dark brown and short.'

'Build?'

'Big. He was big.'

'What was he wearing?'

'Blue jeans and a dark green fleece.'

'Did he have any facial hair?'

'No.'

'Tattoos?'

'No.'

'Was he carrying anything?'

'A waterproof coat.'

'Colour?'

'Dark blue.'

'Did it have a hood?'

'I didn't see.'

'Is there anything else you can tell me about him?'

'Not that I can think of. He seemed painfully shy, I suppose, so I left him to it. Then you rang.'

'Would you recognise him if you saw him again?'

'Oh, yes.'

'Would you mind staying so we can have a look at the CCTV together? You could point him out to me, perhaps?'

'Of course. They've only got it in the foyer though.'

'We'll see him coming and going, at least. Let's go and see if we can find Sergeant Hargreaves.'

They stood up to leave.

'Actually, while I think of it, could you point out Mrs Cromwell to me?'

'Yes. Follow me.'

Dixon and Jane followed Julie back past the nurses' station and into Dyball Ward itself. Eight of the beds were occupied, the first four on either side of the ward, and all of the female patients had had either a new knee or a new hip within the last few days. They stood just inside the doorway and Julie pointed to the first bed on the left.

'That's Mrs Cromwell.'

Dixon looked over to see Mrs Cromwell stirring. She had oxygen tubes in her nose and various pipes and tubes around her bed. She reached across to what looked like a white television remote control and pressed a large red button.

'That's the morphine,' said Julie.

'She's awake,' said Dixon. He turned to Julie. 'Look the other way.'

'But . . .'

'That question you asked me . . .' said Dixon.

'About the beheadings?'

'The answer's yes.'

'I'm just nipping to the loo,' said Julie. She turned and walked back towards the nurses' station.

Dixon looked at Jane. She frowned at him.

'Any evidence is going to be . . .'

'I'm not after evidence, Jane. Just a point in the right direction.'

Dixon sat in the chair next to Mrs Cromwell's bed. He leaned over and spoke quietly into her right ear.

'Vicky?'

She turned her head on the pillow to look at him. Her eyes were glazed over and Dixon could see that she was having difficulty focussing on him.

'Where's Martin?' asked Dixon.

'He's gone.'

She turned away.

'Where's he gone?'

Vicky Cromwell turned her head back to him and looked Dixon straight in the eye.

'He's gone to look for his father.'

Then she closed her eyes and was gone. Dixon watched her for a moment to check she was still breathing. The pause was longer than he had expected but then her chest heaved and she took a deep breath.

⌣

Dixon and Jane walked back out to the nurses' station. Julie Pritchard appeared from behind a door opposite marked 'Staff Only' and Dixon could see a police sergeant approaching along the corridor.

'Anything?' asked Julie.

'Enough,' said Dixon.

'Detective Inspector Dixon?'

Dixon turned to face the police sergeant.

'Hargreaves, Sir. I'm sorry we missed him.'

'Any news on the CCTV, Sergeant?'

'We've got it for the foyer, Sir. You can view it now in the Control Room.'

'I've asked Nurse Pritchard to have a look at it with me so she can identify Cromwell.'

Dixon turned to Julie and nodded.

They followed Sergeant Hargreaves along the corridor and back through the double doors to the top of the stairs. Dixon had thought they were on the top floor, but Hargreaves turned right and climbed a flight of narrow stairs to a small landing. The door off the landing was locked. It had a small window and Dixon could see large steel ventilation pipes on the wall opposite. Hargreaves knocked loudly and a few moments later a security guard appeared behind the window. He looked through the window, left and right, and then unlocked the door.

'This way.'

Dixon followed Hargeaves and the security officer along the corridor. Jane and Julie Pritchard were behind him. They walked in silence, apart from the clicking of their heels on the lino floor. The CCTV control room was at the far end of the corridor. The door was locked but the security guard opened it and stood to one side to let them in.

The room contained twelve screens, all bar one of which were split into four smaller screens. Dixon looked at the screen that was not split and recognised the foyer of the Orthopaedic Centre.

'Is that it?'

'Yes,' replied the security officer. 'I've wound it back to the start of visiting time.'

'Better go back a bit further. What time did he arrive on the ward, Julie?'

'About half past five,' she replied.

Dixon gestured to Julie to sit in front of the screen next to the security officer. Dixon and Jane stood behind them. The security officer wound the film back and then turned to Julie.

'OK, we'll go from here. I'll take it forward at double speed and you sing out when you see him.'

Dixon could see the time stamp in the bottom right corner of the screen: 5.20 p.m. He watched and waited. Various people could be seen coming and going. The footage was grainy, due to the camera quality, Dixon thought, but it could soon be enhanced. He thought also about the last piece of CCTV footage he had looked at and wondered whether this would be the second time he had seen Martin Cromwell on camera. His mind flashed back to a dark night in the Morrisons car park and a knife glinting in the streetlights.

'That's him!' shouted Julie. 'Wind it back, wind it back.'

Dixon looked intently at the screen. The security officer scrolled the film back slowly.

'There he is,' said Julie, pointing at a figure who appeared to be walking backwards around a group of people standing in the foyer. The security officer stopped rewinding the tape and then took it forward until the figure was no longer obscured by the group. He was in the left hand side of the screen, with the camera looking down on him from above. His head was turned to the left and he was carrying a coat in his right hand.

'That's the man who identified himself to you as Vicky Cromwell's son?' asked Dixon.

'Yes,' said Julie.

'Can you zoom it in?' asked Dixon.

The security officer enlarged the figure until he filled the screen. 'Will that do?'

'Yes, that's fine,' replied Dixon. 'What's he looking at?'

'The lift?' asked Julie.

Dixon turned to Jane.

'What do you think, Jane?'

'He's a big lad.'

Dixon tapped the security officer on the shoulder.

'Can I sit there?'

Dixon changed places with the security officer. He sat in front of the screen and stared intently at the image of Martin Cromwell. The screen flickered and the image was, if anything, grainier once enlarged, but he could make out Cromwell's facial features. He squinted at the screen for several seconds before turning to Jane.

'I've seen him somewhere before.'

'What? Where?'

'If I knew that, we'd be home and dry.'

'Recently?'

'Yes, I think so. Give me a minute.'

It was that feeling again. Recognising the actor but not remembering their name or the films they had been in. His usual tactic was to reach for his iPhone and Google it, but that was not an option this time. Dixon closed his eyes. Various pictures flashed across his mind. Sitting in the Dunstan House with Jane. He looked around at the other diners. Nothing. He moved on to the reconstruction. Standing outside Morrisons looking at the crowds on the pavement outside the Pier Tavern. Nothing.

Walking on the beach. The Zalshah. His mind jumped from scene to scene, situation to situation. The Somerset Archive; the Shire Hall, Taunton. He imagined himself standing in court one looking at the faces staring at him. Nothing.

Jane looked at Sergeant Hargreaves and shrugged her shoulders.

Dixon thought about Mrs Cromwell. 'He's gone to look for his father.' He thought about David Selby in the Allandale Lodge Residential Care Home. He opened his eyes. He had a clear picture in his head. He was standing outside Susan Procter's office in the doorway of the kitchen at the Allandale Lodge. He was looking at two carers drinking coffee. Both were leaning against the worktop and wore blue uniforms. One was female. She was laughing loudly. The other was looking at her and smiling. It was Martin Cromwell.

'Gotcha,' said Dixon.

Chapter Ten

It was nearly 10 p.m. before Dixon and Jane got away from the Royal Devon and Exeter Hospital. A panda car had been despatched to Highbridge railway station to intercept Martin Cromwell, should he be travelling home by train. Another was waiting at the bus stop at the top of Pier Street.

Dixon rang the Allandale Lodge Care Home as Jane drove out of Exeter towards the M5.

'This is Detective Inspector Dixon. Can I speak to Susan Procter, please?'

'She's not in now until Monday.'

'Do you have a home number for her?'

'I can't give that out, I'm afraid.'

Dixon did not have time to argue.

'Please ring her and tell her to ring me straight away.' Dixon gave his mobile number. 'Do it now. And tell her this is just about as urgent as it gets. Do you understand?'

'Yes, I'll do it now.'

Dixon leaned across and looked at the speedometer.

'For heaven's sake, Jane, put your foot down.'

Jane accelerated to fifty miles per hour.

'It is a thirty limit, you know,' said Jane.

They approached the traffic lights just beyond the Exeter Crematorium. Jane slowed.

'There's no one there. Keep going,' said Dixon.

Jane muttered something that was lost in the noise of the diesel engine.

Dixon was about to respond when his phone rang. It was a Burnham number.

'Nick Dixon.'

'It's Susan Procter. I had a message to ring you urgently.'

'Yes, thank you, Susan. I need Martin Cromwell's home address and I need it now, please.'

'He's not mixed up in this, is he?'

'I really can't say . . .'

'He can't be. He's such a nice lad.'

'If I could just have his address, please?'

'I haven't got it here. It'll be in my office in his personnel file. Will Monday morning do?'

'No, it won't, Susan. Can you get over there now and ring me with the address as quickly as you can?'

'I can't, no. I've had a few glasses of wine . . .'

'I'll send a car for you. What's your address?'

'It's 36 Westfield Close, Mark.'

'I'll send a car now, Susan. I also need to know when he's due in next.'

'I can tell you that now. He's got the weekend off. His mother was having surgery, he said.'

'OK, we'll speak later. Ring me as soon as you have his address to hand.'

'Will do.'

Dixon ended the call and then rang Bridgwater Police Station. A few minutes later a car was on its way to collect Susan Procter.

'Nothing we can do now except wait,' said Dixon.

'How long will it be?'

'There's a patrol car in Mark now, so it shouldn't take too long.'

———

The motorway was all but deserted as they drove north. There were some wisps of cloud in the night sky now, but Dixon could still see the Plough and Orion. Those were the only two constellations he could recognise and it hadn't taken him long to find them. Next he checked his phone, then his watch and, lastly, the speedometer. It would be almost 11 p.m. before they reached Burnham.

'You got a signal?' shouted Jane.

'Yes.'

They were just south of Bridgwater when his phone rang.

'Dixon.'

'Inspector, it's Susan Procter. I have Martin's address.'

'Go ahead, please, Susan.' Dixon trapped his phone between his right ear and shoulder. He took a biro from his jacket pocket and wrote on the palm of his left hand.

'Flat 5, Cavendish House, The Esplanade.'

'I've got that, thank you.'

'I have his mobile number, if you want that as well?'

'Yes, please.' Dixon made a note of the number. 'Thank you very much for your help, Susan. The car will take you home.'

Dixon rang off.

'Cavendish House, The Esplanande. That's bedsitland, isn't it?'

'Yes,' replied Jane.

'We'll go straight there.'

———

Dixon rang Bridgwater Police Station again and arranged for two uniformed officers to meet them at Cavendish House. They arrived fifteen minutes later to find the patrol car parked along the seafront.

Cavendish House was a large Georgian terrace on the junction of the Esplanade and Sea View Road. He could see that lights were on but he had expected that of a house in multiple occupation.

Jane rang the doorbell of flat 5 just after 11 p.m. The two uniformed officers, both wearing stab vests, were standing directly in front of the door. Dixon stood behind them. They waited. Several seconds passed. Dixon looked at Jane and nodded. She rang the bell again.

'Can I help you?'

The voice came from behind Dixon. He turned round to find himself looking at Martin Cromwell.

'Martin Cromwell?'

'It's not about my mum, is it?' Martin Cromwell's voice was deep and he spoke slowly.

'No. I'm Detective Inspector Dixon and this is Detective Constable Jane Winter. We're hoping you might be able to answer some questions for us.'

'What about?'

'I'd rather not talk in the street, Martin.'

'Do you want to come in?'

'I think it would be better if you came with us to the station, if that's OK?'

'Can we do this tomorrow? I'm tired.'

'I'm afraid not. If you'd just like to go with these two officers, they will take you to Bridgwater Police Station.' The two uniformed officers stepped forward and stood either side of Dixon.

'Bridgwater?'

'Yes.'

'And what if I say no?'

'Then I'd be forced to arrest you but I'd really rather not.'

'All right. Let's go.'

The two uniformed officers escorted Martin Cromwell over to the patrol car, sat him in the back seat and then drove off.

'What do you make of him?' asked Jane.

'I don't know,' replied Dixon, 'but we'll get the police surgeon to check him over before we interview him, I think.'

They got into Dixon's Land Rover and followed the patrol car.

Dixon had taken the precaution of ringing ahead to have the surgeon called out and he arrived at Bridgwater Police Station to find her waiting for him. Doctor Angela Townsend was in her late fifties with short white hair. Crumpled black trousers and a red sweater told Dixon she had dressed in a hurry.

'What have you got for me?'

'That's a long story,' replied Dixon.

'Give me the short version, please.'

'Martin Cromwell. He's the suspect in a multiple murder investigation. We just picked him up and I'd like you to check him over before we interview him.'

'Drugs?'

'I'm not sure. More of a capacity issue, I think. Could be alcohol, could be drugs, could be something else altogether.'

'OK, leave it with me.'

Martin Cromwell had been arrested on arrival at Bridgwater Police Station on suspicion of the murders of Valerie Manning and John Hawkins. He had been checked in and was waiting in an interview room. Dixon left Dr Townsend to it and went in search of the coffee machine. Jane had beaten him to it and was on her second cup when he got there.

'What happens now?' asked Jane.

'We wait for the surgeon.'

Dixon took his coffee from the machine and sat at his desk. He leaned back in his chair and closed his eyes. The next thing he was aware of was a knock at his door.

'Surgeon's ready for us,' said Jane.

Dixon picked up his coffee. It was stone cold.

'Have I been asleep?'

'Half an hour or so.'

They went downstairs to the custody suite where Dr Townsend was waiting for them.

'He's fine, Inspector. He has a very mild intellectual disability, perhaps. And he's hard of hearing. But otherwise he's fine and fit to be interviewed. No drugs or alcohol in his blood at all.'

'I didn't see any hearing aids.'

'He prefers to lip read. And he has some hearing, as well, so he gets by.'

The interview with Martin Cromwell began just before 1 a.m. Dixon made the introductions for the tape and then reminded Cromwell that he was under caution. To be on the safe side, Dixon also gave him the simplified caution.

'I am going to ask you some questions, Martin. You do not have to answer any of them unless you want to. But if you go to court and say something there that you have not told me about, and they think you could have told me, it may harm your case. Anything you do say may be repeated in court. Do you understand?'

'Yes.'

'You have declined legal representation?'

'Yes.'

'OK, let's make a start. Where were you last Saturday night?'

'That's easy. I was at work.'

Dixon looked at Jane then back to Cromwell.

'All night?'

'Yes. I was on nights. Eight till eight.'

Dixon took a deep breath. He drew a large exclamation mark on the note pad in front of him and slid it sideways to Jane with his left hand. He looked back to Cromwell. A change of direction was required.

'Why do you work at Allandale Lodge, Martin?'

Cromwell stared at his hands. He was picking at the skin at the base of his thumbnail on his left hand with the middle finger of his right. He looked at Dixon and then back to his fingers.

'C'mon, Martin. Why the Allandale Lodge?'

He spoke without looking up.

'To be near my father.'

'David Selby?'

'Yes.'

'When did you start working there?'

'Three months ago.'

'When did you find him?'

'Just before.'

'How did you find him?'

'The adoption agency helped me.'

'What happened to your mother?'

'She had a new hip.'

'Your birth mother?'

'She died when I was five.'

'How?'

'She killed herself.'

'Why now, Martin?'

'He's all I've got left, apart from my mum. And he doesn't know who I am. I left it too late.'

175

'What about your sister?'

'Rosie died before my mother. She was ill.'

'Do you know what your father did after that?'

'He was ill too.'

Dixon took a deep breath and exhaled slowly. He felt nothing but pity for Martin Cromwell.

'OK, Martin. That's all for now. We're going to keep you here overnight and then perhaps we'll speak again in the morning. We'll also need to check your work rota for last weekend.'

Cromwell said nothing. Dixon terminated the interview at 1.20 a.m. and Cromwell was taken to the cells for the night.

'What happens now?' asked Jane.

'We go home and get some sleep,' said Dixon. 'Then we get up in the morning, check his alibi and go back to the drawing board.'

Dixon and Jane arrived back at his cottage in Brent Knoll just before 2 a.m. Jane had asked the obvious question and Dixon had spent the rest of the journey brooding in silence.

'If it isn't Martin Cromwell, who the fuck is it?'

It was a simple enough question and it was going round and round in Dixon's head.

Despite the lateness of the hour, he was unlikely to sleep, so he fed Monty and then took him for a walk. It was a cold and crisp night and Dixon could feel a frost forming in the air. He walked in the middle of the road with Monty on an extending lead. He followed Station Road out of the village and into the countryside towards Berrow. He could not recall ever having seen so many stars in the sky. It was one advantage of a late night walk in the countryside, well away from light pollution.

He worked through the cast of characters one by one. Martin Cromwell was still the obvious suspect. He had motive, some might say justification, and was certainly big enough and strong enough. He winced when he remembered the elderly couple at the reconstruction. Nobody in their right mind would describe Martin Cromwell as 'smaller than PC Cole'. Dixon thought about the dark figure wielding the knife when Valerie Manning was taken. It was not Martin Cromwell.

Then he thought about David Selby himself. Vascular dementia would give him the perfect alibi. Dixon did not doubt the diagnosis, but was it possible that Selby was not as bad as he made out? Selby was due to be examined by two psychiatrists on Monday. He remembered the flash of recognition on Selby's face and in his eyes when Dixon had found the old black and white photograph.

Dixon stopped in the middle of the road and looked skyward. What if father and son were working together? Martin could have let his father out of Allandale Lodge on the Saturday night and then back in again in the early hours of Sunday morning.

But was Selby physically capable of it? It might explain the electric carving knife that Roger Poland had been banging on about.

Dixon knew that, apart from checking Martin Cromwell's alibi, very little progress could be made until the psychiatrists examined Selby on Monday. He would need to brief them on his suspicions, but in the meantime, he needed some sleep.

Chapter Eleven

Dixon woke early to find Jane standing next to him with a mug of coffee in each hand. She was naked. He sat up and she passed him the mug from her left hand. Then she sat astride him on the sofa.

'So, what happens now?' she asked.

'We check his alibi and search his flat.'

'No, I meant . . . never mind.'

'What?'

'It doesn't matter,' said Jane. 'What are you doing on the sofa?'

'It was late and I didn't want to wake you.'

'You should have,' she said, smiling.

'Oh, I see. Sorry!' replied Dixon.

'You go steady. A penny dropping from that height could cause you serious injury.'

She leaned forward and kissed him. He reached across and put his mug of coffee on the arm of the sofa. Then he placed his hands on Jane's shoulders and pushed her gently away from him. He allowed the kiss to linger for a moment as he did so.

'Would you mind if we continued this later?'

'I'll hold you to that.'

Jane stood up and then went upstairs to get dressed. Dixon checked his watch. It was 7.20 a.m. He knew that Mark Pearce would be at Burnham Police Station for 8 a.m. so he sent text messages to Dave Harding and Louise Willmott, asking them to be there too. Then he fed Monty.

Dixon was standing at his kitchen window looking out across the fields behind his cottage when Jane appeared next to him. He put his arm around her waist, pulled her towards him and kissed her. Then he whispered in her ear.

'Later.'

Dixon arrived at Burnham Police Station just before 8 a.m. Jane arrived in her own car a few minutes later. The rest of the team were waiting for them in the CID Room.

'Right. Sorry to drag you in on a Sunday but we have a lot to get done. We've got Selby's son by his first wife in custody. Martin Cromwell was adopted in the seventies and only found his father three months ago. He is working at the Allandale Lodge as a carer so he can be near him.'

'A likely story,' said Dave Harding.

'Oddly enough, I believe him, Dave. That's not to say he's not involved, though. He seems to have the perfect alibi for Valerie Manning's murder, but Jane and I will be following that up this morning.'

'Where was he?' asked Pearce.

'At work, apparently, Mark. On the night shift.'

'He could have left and gone back.'

'He could. He could also have let his father out and then back in again.'

'Selby has vascular dementia though, Sir,' said Louise Willmott.

'He does, but do you or I really know how bad it is? He could be putting it on.'

'That would be quite an act,' replied Louise.

'Well, he's going to have to get past two psychiatrists tomorrow, so we'll see,' replied Dixon. 'Now, the son lives at Flat 5 Cavendish House, The Esplanade, which is a bedsit. We need a full search of it. Can you organise that, Mark? Louise, perhaps you would help him?'

'Yes, Sir.'

'Get SOCO there and give it the full works,' said Dixon. He turned to Dave Harding. 'How did you get on with Spalding?'

'I knocked on his door, as you suggested, Guv. You were right. Tenants are in there. They pay the rent to a firm of solicitors in Wells, but obviously I can't speak to them until Monday.'

'What's the name of the firm?'

'Ambrose and Tucker.'

'Check their website and find out who the partners are. If that doesn't work, try the Law Society website. Then go and see them at home. We must find Spalding today, Dave.'

'Yes, Sir.'

'What did we get from the reconstruction?'

'Very little, so far, but it will be on the evening news today and tomorrow.'

'And DNA from the wine glasses in Hawkins' flat?'

'None, Sir,' replied Pearce, 'they'd been wiped.'

'How about a date of death for John Hawkins?'

'Roger Poland is coming back to us with that on Monday,' replied Harding, 'but it won't be with any real accuracy, for obvious reasons.'

'Makes it difficult to check Cromwell's alibi, doesn't it?'

'Yes, Sir.'

'I'll speak to Poland tomorrow,' said Dixon.

'What about Mrs Selby?' asked Jane.

'Let her go. Bail. The usual drill.'

'I'll lay on a car to take her home.'

'No, you won't. She can bloody well make her own way home. She knew full well what her beloved husband had done and kept it secret for over thirty years.'

'Yes, but . . .'

'It's the least she can do. And she'll be doing time for perverting the course of justice, if I've got anything to do with it.'

'Yes, Sir,' said Jane.

'Right then, everyone, you know what you've got to do, so let's get on with it.'

Dixon sat at a computer and logged in. He checked his email and spent the next five minutes deleting messages that were of no interest to him. That left three. The first came from Dave Harding and attached a short wmv file. It was the footage of Valerie Manning's abduction. Dixon clicked on the attachment and watched the film several times. He felt no emotion now, his pity for Valerie Manning tempered by the deaths of Rosie and Frances Southall. They were the real victims. He froze the film with the hooded figure in full view, albeit in profile, enlarged the shot and stared intently at the screen. It was not Martin Cromwell.

'Jane, come and have a look at this.'

Jane got up from her desk and walked over. She looked at the screen.

'Martin Cromwell?' asked Dixon.

'Definitely not.'

'It could be his father, though, couldn't it?'

'Yes, I suppose it could.'

Dixon closed the email. Something was niggling him, but he was not sure what it was. He stared at a blank screen for several minutes before opening the next email. It attached a witness statement that came from the elderly gentleman who had come forward at the reconstruction, Ronald Drayton. He gave a short description of a person wearing dark clothes with a hooded top. He had seen him loitering around the bus stop when he left Morrisons, although, when pressed, he was unsure whether it was male or female. He described the build as slight and certainly smaller than the officer reconstructing the scene.

'You've seen that statement from Drayton, Jane?'

'Yes. Confirms it, doesn't it?'

Dixon went back to the first email and watched the film again. He called Jane over to watch it with him.

'What do you notice about it?'

Jane shook her head. 'What?'

'Watch it again.' Dixon scrolled back to the start of the clip. The figure appeared from behind the bus stop.

'Watch the movement. It's not an old man, is it?'

Jane watched. 'No, it isn't. The movement is too . . . dynamic.' Dixon left the film running to the end.

'Let's have a look at the statements from Selby's other two sons, Richard and . . . ?'

'Marcus,' replied Jane.

'Who checked their alibis?'

'I'll have a look.'

Dixon turned to the last email. It came from Roger Poland and suggested meeting for a beer. Dixon added Poland's mobile number to the list of contacts on his iPhone and then deleted the email. He looked at his watch. It was 8.45 a.m. Mark Pearce and Louise Willmott had left to begin the search of Martin Cromwell's flat. Dave Harding was on his way to Wells.

Jane handed Dixon a copy of Richard Selby's witness statement.

'Dave interviewed him. Simple alibi. He was at home with his wife.'

'Anyone check it?' asked Dixon.

'No. Not yet,' replied Jane. 'It's likely to hold up, though, isn't it? Even if it's bollocks.'

'What about Marcus?'

'He lives in Richmond and was picked up by the Met. He was at a friend's for dinner and it checks out. There are two statements here from a Mr and Mrs Pollard. He was with them all night at their home in . . .' Jane looked at the statement, '. . . Teddington, and left at gone midnight.'

'What does Richard Selby look like, then, I wonder,' said Dixon. 'I've not met him.'

'Me neither. I suggest we put that right sooner rather than later.'

'Good idea. Shall I ring him?'

'No, we'll call unannounced, I think. First things first, though. We need to check Cromwell's alibi.'

Dixon picked up his phone and rang Susan Procter. She was cooking Sunday lunch but could spare him half an hour at 10.30 a.m. They agreed to meet at Allandale Lodge.

'I'll drive,' said Dixon.

Jane threw Dixon's car keys over the bonnet of the Land Rover. He caught them and climbed into the driver's seat. Monty woke up and tried to jump over into the front, but Dixon pushed him back.

'We'll go and see how Mark and Louise are getting on at Cromwell's flat on the way.'

They arrived at Cavendish House just after 10 a.m. A Scientific Services van and two patrol cars were parked outside. The front door was standing open and Dixon could see uniformed police officers and scenes of crime officers in the entrance lobby. Mark Pearce was talking to a man in his late fifties. He had long grey hair tied back in a ponytail and wore jeans and a blue shirt.

'This is the landlord, Sir. Colin Evans. He let us in,' said Pearce.

'Thank you, Mr Evans. That's most helpful of you. I'm Detective Inspector Dixon.'

'You've arrested Martin?'

'We have him in custody at the moment, yes, but I must make it clear that he is not charged with any offence at the present time.'

'I should think not,' replied Evans. 'He wouldn't hurt a fly, that lad. And he's my best tenant. Always pays his rent on time.'

Dixon frowned at Jane.

'I'm starting to see a pattern emerging here.'

'Me too.'

'We'll bear that in mind, Mr Evans, thank you,' said Dixon. He walked past Mr Evans, up the stairs, and stood in the doorway of Cromwell's bedsit. Mark Pearce and Jane followed.

It was a large room at the front of the building, with the same view across to Hinkley Point enjoyed by the late John Hawkins. It occurred to Dixon that Seaview was only two or three hundred yards along the beach.

The room itself was sparsely furnished. There was a single bed along the right hand wall, a table and chairs in the front window and a rudimentary kitchen along the left hand wall. A sofa filled the middle of the room and formed a partition of sorts between the bedroom and the dining area. A television stood on a table opposite the sofa and the bed so that it could be watched comfortably from both.

'Furnished?' asked Dixon.

'Yes,' replied Pearce.

'How much does he pay for this shit hole?'

'Eighty-five pounds a week.'

'Bathroom?'

'Upstairs on the landing. It's shared.'

Dixon spotted Louise Willmott emerging from a walk in cupboard at the end of the bed. She was wearing white paper overalls and plastic gloves.

'Anything, Louise?'

'Nothing, Sir.'

The senior scenes of crime officer, Watson, appeared behind Dixon in the doorway.

'Compared to the last one you laid on, this one's a delight.'

'Have you found anything?'

'Lots of fingerprints, but I expect they'll all be his. Nothing else. And I mean nothing else. Just a few clothes and some wash stuff.'

'He's not planning on staying long, then?' asked Dixon.

'Apparently not,' replied Watson.

Dixon turned to Mark Pearce.

'What's the tenancy length, Mark? Monthly or six months?'

'Month by month, according to Mr Evans.'

'And there are no photos or anything like that?'

'No,' replied Watson.

'Well, we'll check his alibi now. Let me know if you find anything.'

'Yes, Sir,' said Pearce.

Dixon's Land Rover was parked along the Esplanade. He walked back to it in silence. The tide was in and all he could hear was the noise of the water crashing against the sea wall. He looked across to the power station, but his view was obscured by spray and foam rising up from the waves below.

He had no doubt that he would shortly be confirming Cromwell's alibi. Cromwell had gone from victim to prime suspect and back to victim again in the space of eighteen hours. Dixon knew that he too was almost back to square one. Almost, but not quite. He turned and looked back to Cavendish House.

'Poor bastard,' he muttered, but it was lost in the roar of the waves.

⌣

They drove along Berrow Road, turned right into Rectory Road and arrived at the Allandale Lodge Residential Home just before 10.30 a.m. They saw Susan Procter in the car park and so they waited in the Land Rover until she had gone in. A patrol car was parked in the space nearest the front door. It was occupied by an officer Dixon recognised from the search of the golf course. He appeared to be having trouble keeping his eyes open. Dixon tapped on the window. The officer looked up, saw Dixon and then got out of the car.

'You been here all night, Constable?'

'No, Sir. We came on at 8 a.m. PC Cole is on duty outside Selby's room.'

'Seen anything unusual?'

'Nothing, Sir.'

'Good. Well, try to keep your eyes open.'

'Yes, Sir.'

Dixon and Jane walked over to the front door and rang the bell. The front door was locked and was opened from the inside by a carer typing a code into a keypad above the door handle.

'We're here to see Susan Procter. She is expecting us,' said Dixon.

'Would you mind signing in, please?'

Dixon wrote his own and Jane's name in the book. He added his vehicle registration number and 'time in', 10.25 a.m. He noticed that this was the first entry on a fresh page in the visitors' book. He turned the page to glance at the previous entries but noticed nothing untoward. Lots of different residents receiving lots of different

186

visitors. He wondered about those who had received none at all. Nobody had visited David Selby in the previous twenty-four hours.

They followed the carer along the hall, past the dining room on the left and the lounge on the right. They turned right at the foot of the stairs, which were opposite the front door, and then followed the corridor around to the left, past the lift, and into a narrow corridor that led to Susan Procter's office. Dixon took the opportunity to look into the kitchen. This time it was empty.

'Come in, Inspector. What can I do for you?'

Dixon sat in the chair opposite Mrs Procter's desk. Jane closed the door behind them and then stood in front of it.

'We have Martin Cromwell in custody, Mrs Procter.'

'Whatever has he done?'

'He is David Selby's son by his first wife.'

'Good heavens.'

'At the moment he is helping us with our enquiries. We are trying to establish whether he is involved in the recent murders and we need to check his alibi for last Saturday night. Martin says he was at work here, on nights.'

'I can check the rotas easily, Inspector,' said Mrs Procter. She reached down to her right and switched on her computer.

'When did he start work here?' asked Dixon.

'About three months or so ago. I can give you the exact date in a second.'

'Did he tell you anything about himself?'

'Not really. At interview he said he had just moved into the area and that his family was from Exmouth. That's about it.'

'Did he give you a reason for moving here?'

'No.' Mrs Procter looked down and kicked the computer under her desk. She then took hold of the mouse and shook it. 'I'm afraid my computer is a bit slow.'

'I'm assuming you didn't know he was Selby's son?'

'No, I didn't. And Mrs Selby didn't say anything.'

'She didn't know, either. She's never met him and David Selby never spoke of him, apparently.'

'What happened to him, then?' asked Mrs Procter.

'He was adopted as a boy.'

'Poor little blighter.'

'Could David Selby have known?'

'He no longer recognises his wife, Inspector. Let alone a child he's not seen for years.'

'Is it possible that Mr Selby is exaggerating his symptoms, perhaps?'

Mrs Procter shook her head. She was about to reply when Dixon continued.

'I know it's an odd question. But vascular dementia would give him a powerful alibi if he was able to convince everyone that he was incapable.'

'I see what you're saying, but it's impossible. He'd never be able to keep it up for that length of time. And I've certainly seen no sign of it.'

Mrs Procter turned to her computer screen.

'Ah, here we go.'

Dixon watched her eyes scanning the screen and each click of the mouse with her right hand.

'He joined us on 27th July, and . . . yes, he was working last Saturday night. He was on nights, four at a time, so he did Thursday, Friday, Saturday and Sunday. Eight in the evening until eight in the morning.'

'Is there any way he could have left and come back?'

'No.'

'And been away for, say, two or three hours or so?'

'No. Definitely not.'

'Does he have a car?'

'Not that I've seen. He cycles everywhere.'

'What makes you so sure he couldn't have left and come back?'

'Well, he . . . he'd have been spotted by the others on the night shift. It's such a small team they'd know straight away if he'd gone.'

'Who else was on duty that night?'

'Sam, that's Samantha, and . . .' Mrs Procter looked back to her screen, 'Kanya.'

'Are either of them here now?'

'Kanya is.'

'Can we have a word with her, please?'

Mrs Procter picked up her phone.

'Kanya, is that you? . . . Can you pop down to my office for a moment, please? . . . Yes, now.' Mrs Procter put the phone down. 'She's on her way.'

'Let's assume he didn't leave, is it possible he could have let his father out and then back in again without anyone noticing?'

'That would be possible, I suppose, but only if David was capable of it, and he's not. At least, not in my opinion.'

There was a knock at the door.

'Come in,' shouted Mrs Procter.

The door opened and a carer in blue uniform walked in. She was in her early thirties with long straight black hair.

'Kanya is from Thailand,' said Mrs Procter. 'Kanya, this is a policeman, Inspector Dixon, he wants to ask you about the night shift last weekend.'

'OK.'

'Who was on duty?'

'Me, Sam and Martin.'

'What time did you start?'

'We came on at eight.'

'Is it possible that Martin could have left and come back later?'

'What? Gone out, you mean?'

'Yes. For about two or three hours.'

'No. He here all night. I saw him.'

'Was he ever out of your sight?'

'Yes, but not for that long. He answer a buzzer in the night but he not gone for more than ten minutes at a time.'

'Are you sure?'

'Yes. We all sit in the staff room together. All night.'

'Thank you, Kanya.'

Kanya left the office and Jane closed the door behind her.

'Does that deal with it, Inspector?'

'I think it does, Mrs Procter. Thank you for your help and I hope we've not ruined your lunch.'

'That's fine, I'm just glad to help Martin, that's all. He's such a nice lad.'

Dixon turned to Jane and raised his eyebrows.

'We'll show ourselves out, Mrs Procter.'

Dixon walked back along the narrow corridor, past the kitchen. Jane followed. At the end he turned right towards the small table with the visitors' book on it that stood in the hall. It was against the wall between the entrance to the lounge and the front door. Just as he did so, movement to his left caught his attention. He turned to see the lift door closing. He looked up. It was Jean Selby. She had changed clothes and was wearing dark trousers and a black fleece top. She was carrying a red bag in her right hand. It had a long strap and the bag itself was hovering an inch or so above the floor. Her facial expression was blank. She had bloodshot eyes and was looking straight at Dixon but made no acknowledgement of his presence. Then the door closed and she was gone.

Dixon stopped and turned to Jane.

'That was Jean Selby.'

'Didn't see her,' replied Jane.

Dixon stood in front of the small table looking at the visitors' book. He checked the time, picked up the biro and then wrote '10.50' in the 'time out' column. He placed the pen back in the spine of the visitors' book slowly, all the time staring at the left hand page.

'She's not signed in.'

He looked back to the lift and then back to the visitors' book. He turned the page to check the entries for the previous Friday.

'She signed in on Friday afternoon.'

Dixon walked over to the front door. The code for the lock was written in the bottom left hand corner of the Health and Safety sign on the wall to his right. He reached up with his right hand to enter the code into the keypad. He froze. He stood staring out of the stained glass window in the door panel.

'What's up?' asked Jane.

Dixon was staring at a small dark blue car parked next to the police patrol car.

'That car wasn't there when we arrived, was it?'

Jane peered over Dixon's shoulder.

'No, that space was empty.'

'Daniel Fisher's statement . . .' Dixon's voice tailed off.

'A small dark car?' asked Jane.

'Oh, shit.'

Dixon spun round and ran back to the visitors' book. He turned the page and looked again at the previous entries.

'Shit, shit, shit.'

'What is it?' asked Jane.

'What was the name of that firm of solicitors in Wells that Dave said Spalding's rent was being paid to?'

'Ambrose and Tucker, I think he said.'

Dixon read aloud from the visitors' book.

'Friday afternoon: Simon Ambrose. Visiting J Spalding. Time in: 3.55 p.m. Time out: 4.30 p.m.'

'Spalding is here?' asked Jane.

Dixon was already on his way back in the direction of Susan Procter's office. He met her in the narrow corridor walking towards him.

'Julian Spalding?'

'What about him?'

'Where is he?'

'Room twenty-nine. Third floor. Top of the stairs, through the double doors, turn left and he's at the end of the corridor. Why?'

Dixon ignored her. He turned and ran towards the stairs. He shouted to Jane, who was standing in the lounge doorway.

'Get Cole from outside Selby's room. Radio for backup, then follow me up to the third floor.'

'Not Mrs Selby . . .'

'What the fuck is she doing in the lift, Jane?'

Dixon was halfway up the first flight of stairs. Jane looked through the lounge to the corridor of the ground floor annexe that led to David Selby's room. She could see PC Cole was sitting in a chair outside his door. She looked back to the stairs. Dixon had gone.

Dixon ran up the stairs, through the double doors and along the corridor. The door to room twenty-nine was on the right just before Dixon reached the fire exit at the end. Opposite was a fire extinguisher mounted on a wall bracket at waist height. He tried the door to Spalding's room. It was locked. He stepped back, brought his left foot up and kicked the door just above the handle. Nothing happened. He kicked it again. Still nothing.

He turned around and took the fire extinguisher off the wall. Holding the top in his right hand and the bottom in his left, he slammed the end of the extinguisher into the door handle, pulling his left hand away as he did so. The door frame splintered. He picked up the fire extinguisher and hit the door again, just above the handle. The wooden door frame shattered and the door swung open.

Dixon dropped the fire extinguisher and stepped into Spalding's room. The door closed behind him. There was an en suite bathroom to his right, which created a narrow entrance hall of sorts. Dixon took three steps forward into the room itself.

There was a large bay window at the front. He could see Spalding sitting in an armchair in front of the window. Behind him stood Jean Selby. She was holding a long thin bladed knife across Spalding's throat. She pointed the knife at Dixon and screamed at him.

'Stay back!'

Her eyes were bloodshot and her face was red. She was breathing heavily and her nostrils flared with each breath she took. Tears were streaming down her face. The palm of her right hand was facing upwards and Dixon could see that her knuckles were white from the effort of holding the knife.

'It's all right, Jean. Calm down.'

Dixon took a moment to survey the room. He moved his eyes without turning his head away from Jean Selby. The room was large, much larger than David Selby's. A hospital bed stood against the wall to Dixon's right. To his left was a wardrobe, opposite the end of the bed. Against the wall to the left of the bay window was a bow fronted chest of drawers. Dixon could see Jean Selby's red bag sitting on top of it next to what looked like an electric carving knife. In the bay window were two armchairs behind a long low coffee table. Spalding was sitting in the chair nearest to Dixon and was almost sideways on to him.

Spalding himself appeared to be asleep. He looked much like David Selby. He was old, gaunt and slumped in his chair.

'Look at him, Jean. What is the point of killing him?'

'The point?'

'It's more of a punishment to let him live, wouldn't you say?'

'No, I wouldn't!' screamed Jean Selby. 'You haven't got a clue what this is about.'

She replaced the knife across Spalding's throat. He stirred but did not wake up.

'You blame him for what's happened to your husband. David blamed the doctors for the deaths of Rosie and Frances and you blame them for his dementia.'

Jean Selby tried to wipe her tears away with her left hand.

'Look what they've done to him.'

'Look what they've done to you, Jean,' said Dixon.

She began to sob.

'I've watched him tear himself apart for over thirty years and now this. And it's their fault!' she screamed. 'I'm finishing what he started.'

Dixon could hear footsteps coming along the corridor. They were running. Jean Selby pointed the knife at Dixon.

'Stay back.'

Sirens could be heard in the distance. Jean Selby glanced to her left out of the window. She lowered the knife. Not much, but enough. Dixon took his chance. He ran forward, three paces, stepped up onto the coffee table and launched himself at her.

She turned at the last moment and tried to bring the knife back up to meet him. Dixon tried to knock it from her grasp with his left hand as he flew through the air. At the same time, he pushed her head back with his right. He felt a solid blow to his left shoulder.

Jean Selby fell back. Dixon landed on top of her. He tried to get up and found himself kneeling astride her. She was screaming and flailing at him with her fists. He tried to restrain her, but his left arm wouldn't move. He managed to take hold of her left wrist with his right hand and then used his left knee to hold down her right arm.

'You're not going anywhere, Jean.'

Dixon heard footsteps. The next thing he knew, Jane was standing over him. He felt her hands underneath his arms and she dragged him back off Jean Selby. He slumped back against the wall underneath the bay window and looked up at Jane. There were tears in her eyes. He looked across at Jean Selby to see PC Cole holding her arms behind her back and reaching for his handcuffs.

Dixon looked back to Jane.

'Spalding?'

'He slept through it.'

Dixon nodded. He heard the clicking of handcuffs being snapped shut and then the crackle of a radio.

'Control, this is 2562 Cole. We need an ambulance immediately at the Allandale Lodge Care Home, Burnham. An officer has been stabbed.'

Dixon looked quizzically at Jane. Then he looked down at his left shoulder. He could see a black plastic handle sticking out of it and blood pouring down the left side of his chest. He stared at it for several seconds before reaching for the knife with his right hand. Jane reached down and held his hand.

'Leave it,' she said.

Suddenly, the pain hit him. Then he passed out.

Chapter Twelve

Dixon opened his eyes to find Jane sitting on the end of his bed.

'Where . . . ?'

'Weston hospital. A private room. You've had an operation on your shoulder.'

Dixon looked down. The handle of the knife had gone and been replaced with bandages. He tried to move his left arm and winced.

'Don't do that,' said Jane. She moved up the bed and sat next to him.

'What time is it?' he asked.

'Half past eight.'

A nurse walked into the room and stood at the end of his bed.

'You're awake.'

'I am.'

'You've had an operation on your shoulder. The knife has gone, as you can see. I'll call the doctor to have a word with you.'

'Thank you.'

'How are you feeling?'

'Sick.'

'That'll be the painkillers. I can get the doctor to give you something for that. I'll be back in a minute.'

The nurse left and Dixon turned to Jane.

'Where's Monty?'

'I fed him and left him at home.'

'Thanks. Will you . . . ?'

'Of course I will.'

Jane leaned forward and kissed Dixon on the lips. He looked over to see DCI Lewis watching them through the small window in the door.

'Oops.'

'I don't know what you're worrying about. We've all known for ages,' said Lewis, walking into the room.

Dixon pretended to look surprised.

'You forget I'm a detective too,' said Lewis.

'And it's not a problem?' asked Dixon.

'Of course not.'

'Where's Jean Selby?'

'Bridgwater. She's been interviewed and has confessed to the murders of Valerie Manning and John Hawkins.'

'Who interviewed her?'

'I did. With Dave Harding,' replied Lewis. 'She's one angry woman. She blamed them for her husband's illness. The stress of watching his wife and child die, bottled up inside him for all those years. And then she had to watch his descent into dementia.'

'Can stress cause dementia?' asked Dixon.

'Stress can cause hypertension, which can be a cause of vascular dementia, according to Wikipedia.'

'What about Cromwell?'

'Gone back to work.'

'Poor bastard.'

'The doctors tell me there's no permanent damage.'

'That's more than they've told me.'

'You have only just woken up,' said Jane.

'Take as long as you need, Nick. We'll speak next week about your statement but there's no rush.'

'Yes, Sir.'

'I'm working on a traffic case at the moment,' said Lewis.

'Traffic?' asked Jane.

'Yes. Someone crashed into a parked car at Mark last week and then drove off. Failing to stop, failing to report. Serious stuff.'

'How hard are you going to look?' asked Dixon.

'I've closed the case already,' replied Lewis. 'No witnesses.' He got up to leave. He reached into his jacket pocket and produced a packet of fruit pastilles. He threw them onto the bed next to Dixon. 'Put these in your glove box.'

'Yes, Sir.'

'Idiot.'

'Thank you, Sir.'

Lewis stopped in the doorway and turned to Dixon.

'And well done.'

About the Author

Photo © 2013 Damien Boyd

Damien Boyd is a solicitor by training and draws on his extensive experience of criminal law, along with a spell in the Crown Prosecution Service, to write fast-paced crime thrillers featuring Detective Inspector Nick Dixon.

15594664R00123

Printed in Great Britain
by Amazon